A Passing Red

A Passing Red

Lujayne Alqefari

ISBN: 978-603-04-8434-8

To my mother and father
Maryam Alsawi & Abdullah Alqefari.
Thank you for always supporting me and being by my
side.

Special thanks to Dr. Lamya Bin Obaid for pushing me
to start this book and to Dr. Aljazi Alsultan for pushing
me to finish it.

Chapter 1

...

Tap Tap Tap
That is the sound you hear once the devil decides to use you as his little toy.
Tap tap tap
There's no running away from it.
Tap tap tap
Resistance is futile.
Tap tap tap
For the human race is weak, at least that thought is what keeps me sane. The circle of life seems so meaningless when you are a mere spectator, one who does not get brutally dragged down and forced to live through the same torture again and again will not fully understand. Life is a paradox and one can not comprehend this until they're stuck in the middle.
Tap tap tap
I am writing this to teach myself, to warn my future shell of a body, of what is to come and how to survive. By writing my story, I hope to pull the future me out of this hell hole.
Tap tap tap
Those were the sounds of pebbles awakening me from my sleep. Of course, in the beginning I am merely a shell, an innocent human, an incompetent 18 year old girl.
Tap tap tap
It all starts with the taps, the taps of pebbles flying to my window. Signaling the renewal of my prison sentence in this agonizing incarceration, of which I can not guess how long I have been in. It could have been only a week or a 100 years, I am only sure of one thing, that I have to write all that has happened to me thus far, in hopes of pulling myself out.

As I have induced, my actions stay the same each time. Theoretically, by having my writing with me, it will inevitably change my actions. Although, perhaps I have already come to this conclusion before, and yet there is no way to know. Except, I did not wake up with a book, unless I previously failed and in turn have done the same mistake over and over. I can't think of anything else to do so I shall stick to this plan and since I only have a short time left, I will begin the recap now.

As I have previously stated, it started with taps on my window. Followed by my foolish self going to see what the racket was. I had thought nothing of such a strange scene, I allowed my curiosity to get me off my bed and peak through the window.

This most likely will sound like a work of fiction, but what I saw and what has happened to me thus far is real.

A creature, so horrifying, the thought of it makes me want to gouge my eyes out. A beast, like a giant spider who climbed out of the depths of hell, stood there waiting for me. Waiting to renew my pain and suffering.

The first time I laid my eyes upon it, my heart stopped. Time froze. An icy cold hand held me hostage and drugged my veins with pure fear. I could not move nor speak. I wanted to scream my lungs out, call someone for help. However, once eye contact is made, one becomes a mere toy. A weak little rag doll. I could feel my body and yet I had no control of its movement, so as much as I had wanted to run to the other side of the earth, I was but a slave forced to do its bidding.

In this minute of immobility, my eyes were forcefully glued upon the beast. Its body moved in such a strange way, standing in the same spot but moving up and down as if its whole frame were lungs, inhaling and exhaling.

My mind raced to and fro, from sheer panic to utter confusion.

Of course, I had never seen nor heard of such a creature, as most people have not. No sane person could believe such a sickening creature could roam this earth with us. This led me to believe that I was utterly insane, and perhaps I am but in other ways, for I am sure that I am incapable of imagining nor hallucinating such an abomination.

We both stared at each other for what felt like an eternity. All was silent, not even the morning birds sang. The sun was beginning to rise but it seemed distressed, as if something was out of place, as if it wanted to warn the world, to warn me, but could do nothing but pull back her full luminosity. Her light barely cascaded the land, her thick fog danced away in her place, except there was no fog, only the suns warnings.

Suddenly, the creature took a step towards my house door and froze. It stopped rising and descending. At the same time, a sudden urge to go to it popped into my head. That's how it starts. Just a small little thought sent to you by the creature that slowly grows and devours all the logical aspects of yourself. Your sole purpose then becomes to obey.

It was merely a trivial thought but with each second it became stronger. The urge to follow the creature slowly started to course through my veins. I knew that it was wrong and the worst thing I could do in my situation, but I couldn't do anything. It just kept getting stronger and stronger, as if someone was pushing me towards it, telling me it was a life or death situation.

My legs started to move without my consent, taking me outside my bedroom and into the hallway. Sweat ran down my neck as I tried to fight myself, but that part of me became smaller with each step. Unable to fight the urge, the rebel inside me became but a little voice at the back of my head.

My walk gradually turned into a jog, then to a run. My head began to echo with a strong demanding voice,

"**GO TO IT, FOLLOW IT.**" Again and again making me want to ram my head into a wall.

I ran down the stairs, into the hallway, out the door, and stood in front of it. The monster towered over me, baring its razor sharp teeth, urging me to follow it. Then turning around and running off shaking the ground behind it. "**FOLLOW, MUST FOLLOW**" Rang through my head.

I started to run as fast as my feet could carry me, out of my garden, straying further and further from my house. The little voice that still tried to fight, told me that there was still time to go back, but a stronger voice told me to go faster. So, faster I went.

I was mad, absolutely mad and I knew it. Trying to understand what was going on slowly gnawed on my brain, but I could not come up with a reasonable explanation, except that I had developed some sort of psychological illness, something that would cause hallucinations, perhaps schizophrenia. I was convinced that I wasn't mentally stable, yet my legs did not care, as if they had a mind of their own, they hurled me faster than I had ever ran before.

We ran and ran until we reached a meadow, the creature trampled the fully blossomed flowers without giving a second thought. A tragic sight. I wished I could stay in the meadow and collect the poor injured flowers, perhaps I could have revived them or turned them into a perfume, but I could not stop. My legs urgently propelled me forward as if to say there was no time to stop and smell the flowers.

The meadow was covered by a silky grass blanket, so soft each step felt like jumping on a bed mattress. The sun was higher now, though darkness still polluted the air. My legs were beginning to throb and my stomach gurgled. I hadn't eaten anything, in fact, I didn't even change. I looked down at my pink pyjama bottoms, the sheep on them were bouncing up and down with every step, in any other circumstance, I would have laughed at the sight of them. However, the bottom part of my pyjama bottoms were soaking wet from dragging through the field, making them smack and stick to my leg with each step. It was more annoying than you can imagine, as if a cow's tongue were slapping my leg, not that I've ever felt that before.

One step after the other, my legs flew behind the creature, following it out of the meadow. The path slowly started to disappear and more trees were starting to pop up, the more we ran the more would appear, blocking the fragile sun. All would have been dark if not for the few sun rays that somehow managed to find certain places in between the branches to wiggle through.

The trees stood tall and strong, and weirdly resembled giants or ogres, ones who wore full suits of armour. The more I stared at them the more I felt a strange feeling, a feeling I could not explain. It was as if I were looking at real souls instead of weirdly shaped trees. Something about the way they stood, as if they were soldiers waiting for orders seemed rather peculiar.

As I ran, my eyes searched the area but I could not recognise where I was, in fact, I wasn't even aware that there was a forest near my house. It's strange, surely I would have known such a place existed, for I had searched every nook and cranny of the land near my house. As a child, I would roam through the meadow that we had just passed through, imagining I was a princess smelling the flowers in my royal garden. In the winter, I would imagine snow dancing down from the sky to the music of the wind then elegantly lay down on the ground. On the days I would reach the end of the meadow, I would follow the path and it always led me to the village. I was sure that we hadn't strayed off the path yet, I was in a forest and not in the village. It's hard to believe that a forest just sprouted out overnight, but then again, the creature I was following didn't seem plausible either.

I have just realized; I shouldn't write such unnecessary things in this book since I'm not sure how long I can write. I doubt I have much time, so I shall continue my dreaded account while trying to lessen my unnecessary thoughts and memories.

Next, a strange stabbing smell traveled through the air, something that could easily fog your brain. It was as if fragrant flowers and petrol fumes were having a wrestling fight, each trying to pollute the air with its personal smell and in turn, creating a thick fume strong enough to choke someone. My nose fought to understand this strange scent, unable to decide if it smelled pleasant or not.

At the same time, the sound of light tapping started to travel between the trees. I strained my eyes to see what was making the noise but the darkness covered the area like a thick curtain. However, the more I looked at the direction of the noise the more I could make out a shape. There was something in the darkness, it seemed like it was running with us. The light tapping started to get stronger and in turn, the thing ran closer to us. Its silhouette became more and more clear, darting between the trees.

It looked like a dog, but the closer it came the more I started to doubt that conclusion. It was more elegant than a dog, its movements were fluid and soft yet fast. Each step it took graced the ground as if it were a fallen flower, but it could be easily seen how each step was precisely calculated. It wasn't running for the sake of running, it was trying to get to something as if it was a life or death matter.

Once my eyes finally caught sight of the dog-creature, I found it was merely a deer sprinting through the trees. Such a miraculous animal, it isn't easy to look as gentle and as elegant as they are while running with such confidence. Its antlers stood earnestly observing the trees that loomed ahead of it, each twist splendidly complemented the branches above. Its brown fur shimmered each time it passed the few golden rays of the sun. My heart yearned to stop and go up to it, but the urge to chase the horrifying creature was stronger than ever. The deer came so close, that had I turned and ran to it, it would not have had time to run away.

Of course, you'll come to realize that the things I encounter are usually not normal, they tend to be rather bizarre, and this deer was no different. Slowly, it turned its head and looked at me. Its eyes were pools of lava, glowing unnaturally red. A thick red substance stained under its eyes as if it had been crying blood. Though as much as its bloodshot eyes sent shivers down my spine, it gave me a sense of strength and peace. My feet started to slow down, from rapidly running to barely jogging. The deer continued beside me. Two parts of me started to fight, one urging me to run faster towards the monster the other urging me to go back. My brain burned with confusion until my legs finally decided to stop, the deer stopped beside me but the creature kept on running.

I tried to move but the voices were still fighting. **"Chase it. No, go back. Chase it. No, go back."**

My head hurt, an invisible flame traveled through my brain, and without meaning to, a sharp scream escaped my mouth.

It caught the attention of the creature, the deer's eyes boiled red, my heart raced. Although, I shouldn't blame myself for screaming, I doubt that if the same thing were to happen to me now I wouldn't do the same thing. I'm aware that one should not make fun of ones past miseries, and yet doing so makes it feel less real as if everything is just a dream, a nightmare I will soon wake up from.

All I wanted in that moment was the comfort of my mother. I yearned to hear her heartbeat, with my head resting on her chest, as she gives me a hug. I needed her. I needed anyone, anyone to tell me everything was ok. Every speck of blood that flowed through my veins wanted someone to pick me up as if I were just a baby, carry me home, and tuck me into bed. It was too much, everything was too much, I was about to explode, taking the whole planet down with me.

The ground started to shake again, the horrible creature turned around. Its eyes stared coldly at the deer. Then, it started moving towards us, though it seemed to be ignoring my very existence. Turning its head towards me, the deer's eyes glowed redder than plutonium, and weirdly, sorrow seemed to glow alongside them. Never had I seen eyes so apologetic, not even from a human.

Suddenly, a gush of energy pushed me and forced my legs to run back. I truly believed that any minute then my legs would break, I ran faster than I thought was possible for a human. Until the energy abruptly stopped and my legs finally gave in, leaving me sprawled on the forest floor.

Darkness was all I could see from behind my eyelids, exhaustion preventing me from opening them. The ground held me as my body kept me hostage, no energy was present in my body to fight the urge to never open my eyes again. Death seemed so sweet.

__Chapter 2__

Hours probably went by while I slipped in and out of consciousness until I felt a slight spark of energy, enough to get me up. Everything inside of me wanted to just stay on the ground and sleep, but the gurgles my stomach produced compelled me to satisfy it.

I pushed myself off the ground, barely getting into a standing position. Everything hurt, every single bone felt like it had gone through war. I took a couple of steps forward to check my legs but they didn't feel like mine, they felt like imposters, as if a whole clan of leeches had sucked the blood out of them and burrowed into my skin, making it their home.

I raised my head to see where I was and was met with the horrible creature standing in front of me. It moved its body up and down as if inhaling then exhaling its whole body, just like when I first saw it. Its unnervingly human eyes stared through mine, I so badly wanted to run away, but I had no energy left.

It walked up to me shaking the ground with it and opened its mouth wide. Its razor teeth glimmered as they came down upon me. *This is it*, I had thought *death has finally arrived.*

You'd think I'd have been shaking my pants off but surprisingly, I was incredibly calm. I was one with the wind and sky, everything had turned bright in my eyes. The trees that once stood as high and as strong as soldiers were merely laughing children and the darkness that loomed the air were merely black swans dancing under the sun.

How beautiful everything becomes when you face death, except I did not die. The monster's teeth scraped down my neck and attached themselves to the back of my t-shirt. It pulled me up as if it were a cat picking up her kitten.

My feet dangled in the sky, swaying side to side as if a leaf on a branch. The rocks and twigs, that were so plain to see, now were but little ants. Death seemed to have placed its hand upon me so many times that day, being swung around by a supernatural creature did not phase me, either that or I was too tired or shocked to comprehend my surroundings.

Now that I was so close to it, the strange petrol smell became stronger, cancelling all traces of the fragrant flower smell. The more I smelt it, the more I noticed a hint of blood twisting between the petrol smell. It wasn't the type of smell that would make your stomach churn or gag, it was more like the type that sends chills down your spine. Yet, it did not phase me either.

The monster started to walk once again, gripping onto my pyjama top as if I were merely a feather. Left and right, it thrust me through the air. I felt myself slipping, and the neckline of my pyjamas rising to choke me. I held onto it with what little strength I had in an attempt to give myself some breathing space. Had I known what was to come, I believe I would have let myself hang to death. Although, the human body does have a mind of its own, you may want death more than anything, but your body will still fight for survival when faced with it.

Through the forest we went, one step felt like flying over a whole football field. The wind hit us as if to say slow down, but the monster did not care and I could do nothing but try to breathe. On and on we went through the unknown forest, it both felt like the creature had been carrying me for years and merely minutes. I cannot exactly determine how long I was in that situation, as through the journey I was in a state of both wakefulness and sleep. Too tired to be awake but unable to fully sleep while surviving being swung around by a huge barbaric monster.

Suddenly, it stopped and threw me onto the ground, as if I were merely a bin bag being tossed away.

Gravity pulled me down with its mighty force, the ground welcomed me with its open arms, naturally making me gasp with pain. Opening my eyes, I searched for the monster but it was nowhere to be seen. I hoped that now I may return home and forget the whole ordeal, but as I turned my head something caught my eye.

In between the strange soldier-like trees stood an ancient looking tree with bark so patterned it did not seem real, in fact, it seemed as if each swirl and curl was carefully carved by an elite artist who couldn't possibly be human as no human could ever have such a sense of beauty to create such a masterpiece.

Although the tree was smaller than the other trees, it was incredibly more majestic, as if it were a queen in between her royal guards. I feel like it is wrong to call the tree *it*, something about it felt like a living soul.

However, her mystical beauty wasn't what caught my eyes, no it was the door that stood in the middle of the tree that took my attention. It radiated a pastel yellow colour like that of a newly blossomed spring flower, a passionate red swirled the corners of the door making twists and turns ensuring to miss the middle, not taking away too much of the attention from the yellow.

Who on earth would place a door in a tree, was my first thought, followed by *perhaps the tree is hollowed out and is a cozy little hangout spot.*

I liked that idea, so much so I decided to take a quick look inside. My conscience did try to convince me that such an act was incredibly wrong, I had no right to open the door, and yet the idea consumed me. How lovely would it be to have a little hideout in a tree, a place I could run off to be alone or for some peace and quiet. Besides, it wasn't like I planned to steal or pry into someone's life, I simply wanted to get an idea of the place so I could perhaps make my own, that is at least what I convinced myself.

My hand laid on the doorknob, which seemed rather old in comparison to the bright door. Pushing it forward, I was blinded by a strong light, I could do nothing but close my eyes tightly shut. I took a couple steps forward into the hideout whilst my arms shielded what little light it could, and yet I could not see, it was obvious that my eyes had gotten used to the dark outside. I took a few more steps while waiting for my eyes to adjust, totally forgetting about respecting the owner's privacy.

In that state of curiosity, I seemed to have regained a new source of energy which almost completely erased all traces of exhaustion. With my newfound strength, I took a couple more steps, I found it rather weird that I still hadn't reached the end, so I decided to walk till I reached it, except after a minute of walking I realized that there was no way that the little tree could be this big inside.

I opened and closed my eyes and wiggled my face in an attempt to make the light adaption process faster, although I didn't think the funny faces were going to be effective, it did slightly help, either that or it was plain coincidence or maybe even a placebo.

I was still in the forest. Confusion plagued me for the quadrillionth time that day, I was certain I had entered the door. I turned around, realizing the tree had disappeared, vanished without a trace. At that moment, I truly believed with my whole heart that I was not sane and decided that I would go home and phone a doctor straight away. That is, of course, if I could find my way back. *It wouldn't be hard to believe that I'm actually in a psychiatric hospital drowning in a hallucination,* I had thought.

Which, actually, is still an ongoing theory of mine. People who experience such things believe them to be real, only those outside can see if one is truly drowning in madness. However, it's hard to believe my brain has the ability to create all the things I have come upon, and yet the brain is incredibly complex. Who knows if everything is real? Even if I were to find someone to ask, there's a chance they're also a figment of my delusions. Perhaps I'm too paranoid but one must be cautious, especially in such a state.

Chapter 3

I stood silently, my mind roaming to and fro, hoping to find some sort of solution. Everything was still blurry but I could see enough to induce where I was. Except I was no Sherlock, therefore my inductive reasoning was like that of a newborn baby figuring out the world.

As I slowly regained the ability to see under the bright sun, I noticed that there was something strange, the more I focused on certain parts, the more I realized I was not in the unknown forest anymore. The trees were full of lushes green leaves that glimmered and glowed as if they had eternal peace and happiness. They flaunted their bark which had intricate patterns swirled around, it would have been impossible to have them participate in a beauty pageant unless they could all win.

I gently grazed my hand over the grass and was filled with surprise to find it so silky like that of a princess's satin gown. Oh how lovely it felt between my raw hands swimming with flakes and dry patches, each blade soothed my palms better than any moisturiser I owned, which to be fair wasn't many but even so, it felt incredible.

The sun shined brightly upon the flowers bringing them to life and encouraging them to share their fragrance with the air around them, and share they did. Such a delicate smell glided through the air like a ballerina on stage dancing the night away. Such elegance and poise the flowers possessed, it was hard to believe this place was real. The place truly looked like something that had jumped out of a fairytale, an enchanted forest.

At this point, I wasn't really sure what to do, my stomach was begging for food and my legs were pleading to take a break. With no idea how to get back home, I decided that the best course of action was to prioritise finding food and then rest, after that, I'd work out how to get home.

With my bare feet, I walked on the soothing grass which felt heavenly under my beaten soles. However, hunger was slowly plaguing my mind. I was desperate. My stomach didn't understand that there was nothing to eat, so it clung to my nerves like a crying child to its stressed mother.

Lifting my head to the sky in hopes of finding some sort of fruit on the trees, my eyes caught some birds flying through the sky like paint on a blue canvas. Red, blue, and green strokes delicately swam through the air, never had I seen birds these colours except in photos.

My stomach rumbled again and I was teleported out of my thoughts. My eyes wandered between the branches hoping for something, anything that looked edible. On and on I walked pushing through the little energy I had until I spotted a strange little fruit right at the tops of a couple of trees. They hardly looked real, more like something out of a cartoon. Clumped together like grapes, the strange fruit shaped like garlic, shined different shades of pink.

My tongue watered for those strange looking fruit, I'm sure it was only my imagination but I felt like I could smell its sweet scent all the way from the ground. How ardently I wanted to pick one and place it in my mouth. The only problem was there was no way to reach it. The only way was to climb the trees which in my state was near impossible.

I had three options, attempt to climb the tree, continue searching, or sit down and accept my defeat. As much as I wanted to pick the last choice, my spirit refused to just give up and welcome death with open arms. So I decided to crank out my climbing skills.

Unfortunately, the only tree I had ever climbed was a small oak tree when I was thirteen, which I ended up getting stuck, paralysed with fear. My dad had to come and drag me down from it. Funnily enough, the tree wasn't even that big. So as much as I had liked to, it was hard to ignore that I was no expert climber but when one's hunger starts to take over they'll risk all that they know to satisfy the pangs.

My heart started to beat faster as I gazed up the tree. It took an incredible amount of effort to convince myself to place my second foot upon the bark and leave the safety of the ground. I decided it would be best if I don't look down as I heaved my body up from the textured raised part to the next.

How heavy my body felt as gravity worked against me. What usually holds you safely down was now my greatest enemy trying to push me to my death. I knew I was no Olympic athlete but I didn't realize how weak I was, I had barely climbed 1/5th of the tree and I was already out of breath. Although, my hunger and tiredness probably played a part in my breathlessness.

As much as I just wanted to give up, I refused to allow myself to rot without a fight, so I forced myself to go on. Foot after foot, arm after arm until I was halfway through. For some reason, I thought it was totally a good idea to look back and see how much I had climbed and completely ignore the fact that I had thought it was best to not look. Why did I think that was a good idea? My guess is as good as yours.

Looking down, I realized I was further off the ground than I had expected. My blood started rushing through my veins barely able to accommodate my speeding heart, my brain swirled making me unstable. A discomforting ball slowly grew in my chest until it felt like my lungs disappeared as I tried to pull air in. The little part of me that was still strong screamed in my brain to get a grip and hold on tight, but the light started to escape my eyes until my face met the grass below.

Chapter 4

"Oh my, what do we have here?"

A sweet airy voice pulled me out of the unconscious abyss I was floating through. My eyes fluttered open to find the moon illuminating the sky with her darling children, the stars. Trying to find the source of the voice, I used my arms to push myself up, but my body was against me, exhaustion pulled me back down on the ground.

"Oh no, don't move, what on earth happened to you?"

The angelic voice returned, followed by an enchanting girl looking over my face. Her long silver hair flowed with the air and enhanced her incredibly pale face which was as clear as ice. She had eyes like that of a mystical fairy, glowing as if they were two small purple stars, a lighter shade in the middle that got deeper as it reached the ends of her iris. I didn't even know such an eye colour was possible, but there she was, her purple eyes wide with sympathy and compassion.

I opened my mouth in an attempt to speak but no sound escaped, my throat was dryer than the Sahara Desert. "No no, you're in no state to move or talk, Alleta go get some guards and the medic."

My ears lit with relief hearing those comforting words but were interrupted by pangs of pain in my head, and the aches through my body started to torture me once again. My eyes became heavy and life became blurry until I was back in the unconscious world where time does not exist.

My memories of the next couple of hours are blurry as I was in a state where I drifted in and out of consciousness. I can vaguely remember being picked up and taken somewhere but that's about it.

I then woke up suddenly, going from the world of sleep to reality in a heartbeat. However, I didn't know what had happened nor where I was. My heart pounded and adrenaline rushed through my veins but my mind was empty.

I found myself in a bed, so soft and comfortable, it gently massaged my sore body. I passed my hand over the silky duvet and let out a sigh of relief *yesterday wasn't a dream, yet I am alive*, I had thought. All the confusion flew away, allowing my mind to become organised once again, although a slight sense of shock and disbelief was still present in me.

I then realized that I hadn't the slightest idea as to where I was. Picking my body up into a seating position, doing my best to ignore all the aches, I found myself in a rather big bedroom. The sight of it left me in awe, to think that such a room existed on this earth, let alone this day or age, was astonishing. The room truly looked like something out of an enchanted castle in a fantasy novel.

A huge arched window, covering 90% of the wall in front of me, revealed a breathtaking garden so large I couldn't see the end. My eyes roamed over the magnificent sight of the marvelous trees and the delicate flowers. I reveled the sight of the delicate tulips, the lavish roses, elegant orchids, and all the flowers that I could not distinguish. It seemed there was an endless amount of them living in the garden.

A clear stream wiggled here and there flaunting its cascading water, it was a symphony conducted by nature. Gazebos adorned with bright green leaves and dazzling flowers scattered through the land, complemented by dainty little birds resting upon them. The window contained a masterpiece, if not for the frolicking birds, I would have been sure that it was a painting of a fictional garden.

After delightfully observing the garden, I allowed my eyes to examine the rest of the room. Fancy pillars with intricate detailing adorned the corners of the room, around the arched window, and the fireplace, all was a soft cream colour. A long dusty pink sofa and two lavish chairs of the same velvety material sat in front of the window upon a fancy cream carpet fit for a king. Apart from the hardwood floor, everything was either a creamy white or pale peachy pink, the two colours along with the brown hues of the floor perfectly complimented each other. There is no way I could perfectly describe the amount of elegance the room contained nor how grand it was.

I laid myself back down, allowing my head to sink on the soft pillow. Not knowing what to do with myself, I decided to live in the moment and take advantage of the calmness and tranquility that I had, not long ago, passionately wanted. All was silent but my steady heartbeat as my eyes watched the ceiling, my mind and my bones soaked the serenity that seemed to flow through the air. My eyes began to get heavy and sleep washed over me like an ocean wave.

Although it had felt like I had just slept for a couple of minutes, my eyes were greeted with the sight of utter darkness, if not for the little lamp that sat on the nightstand. I noticed curtains hiding the spectacular view of the garden and a tray with a round silver cover sat on the table. Had my body been so desperate for rest that it ignored all signs of disruption?

I wiggled my feet to see if they were ready to be of use, although they ached quite a bit, they seemed strong enough to allow me to walk around the room. Getting off the bed, I crossed the room to the window and peeped behind the curtain. The moon was high in the sky, once again, with the stars. They lightly illuminated the garden below, causing it to look more enchanting than the first time my eyes laid upon it.

How I wished to forever stay in that position, to not have to leave that particular time, for at that moment everything felt right, as if no harm could get into the tranquility of the second. If only that were possible, I wouldn't doubt that the sight of the garden would have occupied my mind for years, eliminating all thoughts of boredom. However, that is not how life works, you can't stop time, you are forever forced forward, and so forward I went.

Despite the fact I wanted to search the rest of the room, my body began to warn me of its weariness, so I propped myself onto the long couch. In front of me was the table with the tray and metal covering on top, I took it as a sign that whoever took me here placed some food for me.

As I picked the cover off, the most heavenly aroma wafted through the air, announcing the presence of a perfectly seared steak. The aroma danced around teasing my rumbling stomach, I could have easily eaten the air surrounding me. Once my eyes caught sight of the steak encircled by a mixture of lightly roasted vegetables, I was reminded of how long I hadn't eaten. I began to shake, sweat ran down my neck, the sight of the food made me weak with hunger.

The first mouthful of steak, although slightly cold, felt sensational on my tongue. I devoured the whole plate as if I were a ravenous wolf. Barley chewing each bite, I shoved them down my throat piece after piece. Five minutes and the plate was clearer than my own future.

Eating after a long period of hunger is such a peculiar sensation, it opens your mind to how truly weak and vulnerable we are. We believe ourselves as the kings of earth, the superior specie, and yet a day or two without food brings us to our knees. Only when one feels hunger, does one realize how thankful they should be. To think that there are people without the certainty of having food for the day, or that they live their lives with their stomachs begging for something to fuel their body, makes me forever thankful for being fortunate enough to not have to worry about such things on a daily basis. It was then that I realized my life was perfect before yesterday, although I never complained about my life, I never fully understood how thankful I should have been for it.

We tend to look at those above us, we don't realize how lucky we are until we experience something below what we are used to. Perhaps if we looked at those below us instead we may enjoy life better. Life is incredible and worth more than anything one could think of, why should we spend our time comparing ourselves to those on top?

As I mused over these topics with the satisfaction of a full stomach, I fell asleep once again.

Chapter 5

Knock knock

I returned to the world of consciousness once again, awakened by a knocking at the door. A petite lady walked in with a little trolly, her eyes glimmered orange like two giant gems complimenting her long, thick, orange curls. It wasn't ginger but a mixture of eye catching hues ranging from a soft pastel to an intense vivid orange.

"Um, hello." I said, confused at the random entrance.

Turning to face my bed, her long black dress swished alongside her, accompanied with the white apron she wore.

"oh, your awake." Her eyes widened, displaying such innocents as if she were a child stuck in an adult's body.

"Yes, who are you?"

"I do not have permission to give you that information." She answered without much emotion.

"Uh, well then where am I?" I asked, confused at her reply.

"I do not have permission to give you that information."

My attempt to garner information was completely thwarted. The first person I see in this room refused to tell me anything. However, I wasn't ready to give up.

"Then who can I ask? Please I need answers." I tried again.

"The princess."

What? I didn't understand. The princess? *Was this a joke?* Although, it did explain the grand room and the majestic garden.

"The princess?" I asked.

"Yes."

"well, how can I meet her?"

"I do not have permission to give you that information."

She was starting to tick me off, her answers gave me little information, affecting my mood.

"However," she started again "her majesty has requested to see you once you are fully healed."

With this information, my irritation began to boil down. In fact, I was ecstatic, *I get to meet a real princess?* Yet there was a nagging sensation that told me everything, so far, was too good to be true. Why would a princess want to meet me? I was nothing special compared to the people I had seen so far. Not that I had seen many.

Still, to compare myself to the two people I have seen so far would be to compare a mere sketch with a masterpiece. So far, all their eyes glowed with enchanting colours and, for reference, mine were but oceans of twilight. Their cascading hair flowed and danced with the wind, but mine lived lifelessly by my chin. It was true that my hair swirled with waves and curls but so rarely did it sit right that it would be insulting to compare it to the orange curls of the women I had just met. Not to say I'm hideous or anything, I've always thought I was pretty, but incomparable to these people.

The women started to dust the walls, her curls moved behind her so enchantingly, it was hard to keep my eyes off her. Since she wasn't going to give me her real name, I decided to refer to her as maple, as her eyes and hair reminded me of a maple tree in autumn.

At this point, I had no idea what to do, so I thought it would be a good idea to nag maple for some more information.

"Hey, can I meet the princess now?" I asked

"No."

"But I'm healed."

"Not fully."

She was right I still had aches and pains travelling through my body but only enough to cause annoyance.

"I only have slight pain though."

She didn't answer. *How rude.*

"Well, which way is the exit?" I tried again.

At this, she stopped and turned around to face me.

"Y o u are not permitted to leave." She answered sternly.

"I beg your pardon?" I blurted out. "Why on earth do I need permission to leave?"

"You may not leave until you meet the princess, she will decide your fate."

My fate? All I asked was where the exit was, what does my fate have to do with anything? These people seemed rather strange.

I then continued to watch Maple wipe the already gleaming window and sweep the already spotless floors. Not a speck of dirt could be found, yet she bustled around as if the place hadn't been cleaned in a century.

At long last, she stopped and pulled a tray out of her trolly. Another metal plate. She placed it on the table and left without a word.

Indeed she was a strange woman, yet I was glad to have met her. I felt less isolated, however, my curiosity was not put out, rather it was amplified as if someone had tried to put out a fire using gasoline.

I got up and went to the couch while pondering on what little maple had said. As I picked up the metal lid belonging to the metal plate, I wondered why she seemed so innocent and showed so little emotion.

Delicate little sandwiches were gracefully placed upon the plate and yet they took none of my attention, too many thoughts occupied my head. I mindlessly started eating, wondered why her hair seemed to glow. Every part of her was strange but something about her hair was most peculiar. Something about it was abnormal.

Chapter 6

A few days passed without much happening. Maple would come to clean and bring me food, while I would ask an endless number of questions but to no avail. Until a week from the day I first came. Maple entered the room at the same time as usual however, she did not have her trolly. "You shall meet the princess tonight." She pronounced.

Everything seemed so strange but what was stranger was my willingness to play along. I knew I was to meet her sometime sooner or later, yet I was lost for words. There were no introductions nor explanations. I didn't even know who the princess was yet I was to meet her tonight. How incredibly bizarre.

"Four maids are waiting outside for you."

"Four maids?" I asked, "why are four maids needed to take me to the princess?"

"They shall not be the ones to take you to her highness, they have been picked to get you ready to be in her presence."

Four maids to get me ready? What on earth were they planning to do with me? All I thought was necessary, was to take a quick shower, but surely they believed I was capable of that on my own. I wondered if perhaps they were worried about my injures, that made the most sense, and yet it still did not justify having four maids.

She then left. Whenever I was ready? There was nothing I could do apart from sleep or watch the garden, so I decided to not waste any time. I hurled myself off the bed and went to wear my shoes, except I had no shoes, I didn't wear any when I ran out of my house. *Was it appropriate to leave my room without any?* Well, it wasn't like I could summon up some sort of magical shoes, so off I went to the door.

As I placed my hand on the doorknob I took a last look at the room behind me. The garden truly couldn't bore my eye, every second it seemed to become more charming. I decided then that the first thing I'd ask of the princess was to let me roam the garden.

The door calmly pushed open revealing four ladies wearing the same uniform as Maple. "Hello." I beamed.

One of the ladies, a slender girl with short black hair and eyes darker than midnight, sneered. The one next to her swished her head and looked at her with warning eyes. Looking back at me, she half smiled "Hello, please follow us."

I would have listened to her command, if not for the fact I had noticed the sneering lady had ears like a cat, another one of the ladies had them too. At first, I thought they were headbands but then I noticed swishing tails behind both of them.

As I stood at the doorway, utterly perplexed, the lady spoke again "I apologise. let us introduce ourselves, I am Akhthar," she said as she pushed her green hair behind her ears.

Pointing at the sneering lady "Mau," then the other cat lady "Thal," and lastly a short ginger haired girl "Asal."

My mind was occupied, they had tails and they moved the way real cats moved theirs. Proudly standing, it was as if they genuinely had feline souls, divinely prowling around as if mocking me for the lack of feline blood. *Could it be possible that they truly were cats? Impossible and yet how many impossible things had I encountered thus far?* It would have been absolute folly to have fully convinced myself it wasn't true.

"What are you staring at li…" Akhthar clapped her hand over mau's mouth and said " I apologise please follow us"

"No wait, li what?" I asked.

Turning around and walking off, she replied "Nothing, Mau is just incredibly ill mannered."

I couldn't think of any inappropriate words beginning with li, so I chalked it up as one of the country's slang.

I followed behind Akhthar and Asal, while Mau and Thal prowled behind us, the former snickering away like a horrible teen the latter quiet but I could imagine a sly smirk painted across her face.

Akhthar, her back straight, marched with the confidence of a leader. Her green hair, slicked back, unmoving with every step. While, short and stout, Asal seemed like a lump of clumsiness besides Akhthar, but she confidently mirrored her every footstep, as if they had planned how to walk beforehand.

We walked through the fancy halls, the morning light streaming in from the many tall windows, although incomparable to the height of the walls, adorned with fancy cream pillars. My eyes were invited by the beauty of the chandeliers that shimmered through the hall. Each one begged my eyes to roam upon them, to indulge their splendour.

Stopping in front of a door, Akhthar knocked gently. It slowly opened revealing a burning lady, the size of my palm, flying at the door. My eyes widened, *what on earth is that?*

"Hello," her velvety voice encompassed the silence "aren't you a strange thing." She said as she poked my nose.

"I'm the strange thing?" My eyebrows furrowed with confusion.

"She speaks?" Her eyes widened, shock took over her voice as she faced Akhthar.

"They all speak" mocked Mau a smirk plastered on her face.

"You know what I mean." The little lady scowled.

"Mau if you open your mouth one more time I will inform the boss of your actions," Akhthar growled then gave a warning look to the flying creature, who innocently shrugged. Turning back to me with an exasperated smile, she continued, "This is the keeper of the guest changing room," She pointed at the little burning lady who flew and elegantly sat on her finger.

Was I suppose to know what a keeper was? My mind was going to explode with bewilderment, nothing made sense anymore. My eyes darted around me trying to make sense of the two cat ladies, the crazy coloured hair, and the little burning lady. *Where was I?*

Chapter 7

Minutes later, I was set into a warm bath. I hadn't realised how much I needed it, every inch of my skin and bones basked in the warmth. I was in a blissful cocoon, the water washing away the past. That is until the little flying thing, who turned out to be called Nara, snuck behind me and heaved a whole bottle of shampoo on me.

"HEYYY," I shouted trying to stop the shampoo from reaching my eyes "WHAT ON EARTH ARE YOU DOING!?"

"You stink," she replied.

I didn't doubt it, considering the past few days, but she didn't have to be so frank.

"You know I can shower myself," I puffed as she danced on my head spreading the shampoo with her feet.

"I wouldn't be surprised."

"And why would you be surprised in the first place, do people not know how to shower here?" I rolled my eyes.

"Well considering your species…." She stopped in her tracks.

"My species what?"

She feigned a laugh as Asal burned through her with her eyes.

"You know Asal is a shifter." Nara changed the subject.

"A what?"

"You don't know what a shifter is?"

"No?"

"Huh, where on earth was she found?" Pointing at me, she asked Asal who simply replied with a shrug, "you are rather strange," I wasn't sure if that was directed to me or Asal.

"Well, what on earth is a shifter?" I asked as she started dancing on my head again.

"Considering you don't know anything, I don't think I'm allowed to tell you, but then again I'm not one to follow rules," bending down from the edge of my head, her burning eyes met mine, a sly smile plastered on her face. "A shifter is one of the species of intelligent beings who can shift, Asal is a penguin shifter."

"Shift as in shape shift?" I rolled my eyes

"Ooh, you are clever," she stood up again going back to working in my hair.

I wasn't sure if she was serious or not. On one hand, I had seen enough unexplainable things to believe it, one being the small fire creature that was skating through my hair, but to shape shift you'd need to change your whole body, your DNA, it didn't seem plausible. "Can you show me?" I asked Asal as she poured warm water over my feet, washing off the soap, only leaving behind the delicate scent of lavender and roses.

"No," she replied.

"Your so boring Asal," Nara groaned.

I knew it, impossible.

"You know Mau and Thal are shifters too and they're not as boring as Asal," She babbled on, "so they'll show you."

"The two pretentious cat girls?" I rolled my eyes again.

Nara stopped shaking around on my head and threw her head back with laughter, "well they are cats after all."

Now that, I could believe.

"Speak of the devil," Nara flew off my head and flew to the doorway, her feet dripping soap all over the floor, "guys please turn into cats," she whined.

"Why?" Scowled Mau.

They didn't have to shift for me to believe they were cats, their mere attitude was enough proof. By simply standing, they filled the room with the self confidence and pride that only a feline could possess.

"She doesn't know what a shifter is," Nara pointed at me.

"*It* doesn't know what a shifter is?" Mau's eyes filled with amusement, a mocking smile appeared on her silent friend's face. Their eyes met, confirming their thoughts, then both placed their hands down like a stretching cat and shifted to pure felines in a matter of seconds.

My mouth dropped, *how on earth?* I couldn't be more at a loss for words.

"Yay," Nara squealed like a child "they're so adorable aren't they?" Flying down to pat Mau, who replied with a hiss.

On the white marble floor, Mau's pure black fur seemed to suffocate the light around her. Her once brown eyes, glowed a deep golden shade against the darkness of her feline body. Besides her, Thal stretched out, completely unaware of the stark difference between them. Her pristine white fur blending in with the floor, inviting the sunlight spilling from the windows to shimmer through her fur. The ocean seemed to reside in her eyes, lightning booming through them, erasing what once was dull grey.

As Mau hissed at Nara for even considering petting her, Thal elegantly propped herself on one of the windowsills. Basking in the sun, it was as if she and the rays were one. Her eyes drooped and her muscles began to relax without a care in the world. A true cat.

Meanwhile, Mau had realized that there was no way of stopping the burning creature from petting her, unless she took some drastic action, but instead opted to shift back to her human form.

"The amount of skill you possess to annoy someone far exceeds your size." Mau nearly spit in Nara's face, who simply replied with a hmph.

As she was about to fly over to Thal, someone knocked on the door. The green haired lady, Akhthar, entered. Nara stopped in her tracks, pretending to grab some type of bottle near the windowsill. No one spoke.

"Akhthar, heyyy, we are nearly done here," Nara rattled off as if she was as innocent as a newborn child.

Akhthar's black eyes gleamed, turning a shade darker than I thought possible. I wanted to ask if she was a shifter as well, but I knew better.

Everyone working uniformly, tensions bounced off the room. A jug of water came splashing down on my soapy hair, harsher than was needed. As I looked back to glare at Nara for being rough, the snickering eyes of Mau mocked my annoyance. I grimaced, of course, the little lady wouldn't be able to hold a jug that size. Another harsh splash of water, and a slight giggle you could barely hear, grazed my ear. Every second my hatred grew for the strange cat who seemed to hate me for no apparent reason.

Washed and dried, poked and prodded, I was finally ready. I looked in the mirror, a girl stared back at me. We looked both alike and yet completely different. Of course, my face did not change but everything else had. Instead of my stained pyjamas, a dress sat upon my skin as soft as a petal, stretching down, slightly above my ankles. Its bluish grey colour resembled nothing that I had ever seen before. The dress was not fancy, rather it was simple, and yet the way it delicately sat upon my frame made it seem as if it was made of magic.

My messy curls had been pinned back, a few strands left, framing my face. A pair of simple flats, the same shade as the dress, felt like a second skin upon my feet. "What now?" I asked the maids who crowded around the mirror.

"We wait." Replied Nara.

"For?"

"For the time."

"What time?"

"The time to meet her highness, you can't just randomly go see her," She rolled her eyes.

I didn't think of that, which gave me the idea to get a feel of this place while we waited. "Are there any other beings apart from shifters and whatever you are?" I asked.

"Of course silly, you've got shifters, elves, chimeras, the four dima's..."

"The four dima's?"

"Well, technically there are five."

"Nara," Asal warned.

The number of times they warned each other began to seem suspicious. "What are the five dima's?"

"Four," Asal growled

"Ok then, what are the *four* dima's?" I corrected myself.

"There are four groups of beings who look like your species, but have one of the four elements of nature flowing through their blood," Nara replied.

I didn't understand one bit and it showed on my face.

Mau scoffed, "don't waste your time they're incapable of complex thought."

"I beg your pardon?" I turned around, she laid carelessly on the large window sill, flicking her tail side to side as if begging to be slapped.

"Mau stay in line," Asal warned.

Without a reply, Mau simply closed her eyes, a mocking smile painted on her face. How passionately did my hand want to wrap around her pretentious tail and rip it right out of its socket.

"Anyways," continued Nara, "there are way too many species of intelligent beings for me to count all of them off for you."

"Well how about everyone here? Are you a fairy Nara?"

Her eyes widened, utter disgust plastered her face, she seemed to burn harder and brighter "do I look like a fairy?"

"Oh no, I didn't mean to offend you, it's just the only small humanoid creature that I have heard of that can fly are fairies."

Mau began rolling in laughter, "Nara the humanoid fairy," she mocked, her hand placed on her chest to calm her rapid breathing as if she had heard the funniest joke.

"BE QUIET!" The little creature screeched, " I am no human nor fairy," she took a deep breath before replying to me "I am a fire pixie, fairies have wings and are abhorred by all for their vile behaviour."

"Oh, I'm sorry," I replied.

As Mau calmed herself, Akhthar reappeared, "The princess awaits you."

Chapter 8

A grand door stood in front of me, an invitation to see what was to come of my future. I took a last look at Akhthar, who had led me there. She gave a nod of confirmation. The doors slid open as I gently pushed them in.

I found myself in a huge dining room, big enough to welcome a village. Huge windows actively welcomed the midday light which shone upon the long fancy table. Standing at the front was a gorgeous woman with a glowing smile plastered on her face. The woman with the purple eyes.

She wore a long lilac dress which made her eyes seem to glow against her glassy skin. Her sleeves, slightly puffed, came down slightly above her elbows, enhancing her sleek pale arms.

How was I supposed to great a real life princess? I decided to curtsy. As I looked back up, I became mesmerised by her purple eyes which seemed to encapsulate a soul of pure kindness. It was as if they spoke, telling me that their owner was someone who saw only the sunshine of others.

"No need to curtsy," her soft voice elegantly danced, "I am Ashta."

"It's very nice to meet you princess Ashta."

"Please, don't call me princess," she rolled her eyes with a charismatic smile, "and you are?"

"Lana," she was the first person to ask for my name.

"It's very nice to meet you, Lana, please sit."

"Were you the one who saved me in the woods?" I asked as I sat down.

"No, I just found you, the medics did the rest."

Two people entered the room, both holding trays, a sweet aroma entered the air. A mixture of honey and freshly brewed tea. They lay upon our side of the table a mixed array of cakes and pastries, then served two cups of tea.

"Thank you," we both chimed.

They bowed their heads and left.

"So, Lana, where are you from," her eyes shone with genuine curiosity as she drank her tea.

"The Middle East."

"So you are from here?" She asked in confusion.

"No, I don't know where I am, but this couldn't possibly be the Middle East."

"But it is."

"What?"

"This is the Middle East governed by the buna-fsiji family of ice dimas"

"But... that doesn't make sense," I stuttered, fear of never going back home beginning to etch itself into my veins.

"How so?"

"Well, first of all, the Middle East, *no the whole planet*, doesn't have strange humans that transform and fly and whatever else you guys are capable of," I found myself standing as I rambled, "I apologise, it's just that I fear I've gone mad, there is no one like the people here where I'm from," I said as I sat back down.

"I don't quite understand, however, I deeply sympathise with your situation," she smiled sadly, compassion swimming through her glowing eyes.

We both sat in silence, munching away at the cakes and pastries. I would like to say they tasted divine, but with my mind racing a million miles a second, it's a miracle that I remember what I ate.

"So, correct me if I'm wrong, you come from a place where only humans exist?" The princess started up again.

"Yes, we'll technically no, there are animals but no intelligent beings apart from humans, wait are you saying you're not human?"

"No," she chuckled softly " I am a dima."

"Oh, I guess that makes sense."

"Lana, I want to help you get home."

"Why?"

"I don't know," she smiled and looked up, "I just feel like it's the right thing to do, besides a world with only humans? How strange."

"I believe a world with a mixture of strange beings, is far more strange," I replied.

We returned to eating silently, a sense of serenity flushed through me. I had help, I wasn't alone anymore.

"What makes a human and a dima different?" I asked.

"Well, some people believe humans are dima's too, but most people disagree," she replied.

"How so?"

"Well, it's hard to explain but," she sighed, "humans look like dima's, but what makes them different is that we have elements of nature in our blood."

"I've been told this previously but I still do not understand."

"There are four types of dima's, the earth dima's, the water dima's, the fire dima's, and me, an ice dima."

"And air dima's?"

"Air dima's?"

"The four elements of nature are earth, water, fire, and air."

"I can't say I've ever heard of air being part of the elements, except in stories."

"Oh, where I'm from, ice isn't part of the four elements."

"But if you come from a world of humans. How do you know about the elements?" Ashta asked frowning.

"Well I'm not quite sure of the history, I think the ancient Greeks invented the idea that everything was made up of the four elements, but people commonly know about it from fiction."

"Oh," she replied as she sipped on her tea.

"So is there actually ice in your blood?"

"Mhm," she nodded.

"Well, our blood just has blood, why do people think we're dima's?" I asked

"That's why people don't think your dima's," she said as she set her teacup down, "humans have plain blood, but some people believe that they have the ability to suddenly possess amounts of speed and strength that they didn't previously possess. Is this true?" She asked looking deeply into my eyes.

"Maybe if they had superpowers," I chuckled.

"That's what I thought," she smiled.

"Why didn't you just ask a human before?"

"Humans are rather rare."

"Why?"

"I don't know, they just are."

Humans possessing sudden power, unless humans here are different to me, it definitely is untrue. Perhaps people here believed in super-powered humans the way humans back home believe in aliens.

The sunlight began to lose its morning brightness, reminding me of what I wanted to ask the princess, "can I see the garden?"

"Sure... we can go now if you like," she said with a warm smile, "oh, I nearly forgot, wear this."

she handed me a shining medallion shaped as an intricate snowflake the size of my palm.

"Why?"

"It's the sign of being a guest of the buna-fsiji family."

"And?"

"It allows you to freely roam the palace without a chaperone, except of course the prohibited areas, those can only be entered by family," she grinned, "oh, and never take it off."

"Why?"

"You say why a lot," she chuckled, "it will keep you safe *and* allow you to obtain necessary items free of charge, *THAT MEANS YOU CAN EAT TWENTY CAKES IN A DAY AND NO ONE CAN STOP YOU*," she excitedly boomed as she stood up.

"Can you not eat twenty cakes here?" I laughed as I wore the necklace.

"Ugh, I can't, my diet is monitored," she rolled her eyes "*but,* that doesn't mean one can't disguise themselves and wear a royal medallion," she winked with a cheeky smile as she began to walk to the door.

Chapter 9

To compare the garden to a wonderland would perhaps be insulting, for it was more like heaven on earth. A lake that flitted here and there glowed a mystical aquamarine blue, enchanting the princess as she walked beside me. Her purple eyes shimmered as they looked at the luminescent lake.

"This is my favourite part of the garden," she said as if in a trance.

"Why is it glowing?" I asked.

She smiled at me as if I was a curious little child, "well, I'm not quite sure, but you could ask the garden keeper."

We walked forward by the lake, trees of different shades of green and purple dangled above us, the bottom of their trunks adorned with dazzling wildflowers. It seemed to be mother nature's loving home, a place in which a sense of serenity and understanding flowed naturally between me and the princess. We didn't talk much, we didn't need to. One look, one smile, one gesture, was enough for us to understand each other. A connection that I had never felt before existed between us, as naturally as the gentle clouds that swam above us.

We continued our silent journey in perfect understanding and synchronisation. The sounds of the trees and flowers rustling as the little creatures pranced around, filled the air alongside the bird's graceful singing.

"I've been thinking," started the princess, "to find your home, we probably have to visit the location you were found."

"Mhm."

"Do you know how you got there? Or perhaps, did something unusual happen before you found yourself here?"

I cringed as the horrid memory rushed back to me, "I chased a giant spider thingy and found a tree with a door."

"Did you enter it?"

"Yeah," I sighed, crinkling my nose at my utter stupidity.

"Ok, well that's a start, how big was the spider *thingy*?" She grinned, mocking my horrible description.

"Hugeee, like the size of three elephants standing on each other or something," I said as I waved my arms, mimicking its size.

"Huh, that's weird, we only have tiny spiders here."

"We don't have huge spiders, that's why it's so unusual."

"Oh?" Her eyebrows rose, "Then why would you chase it?"

"I- I don't know."

She stopped in her tracks, her purple eyes squinted with confusion, "You don't know?"

"I don't know, I just had to," my brain began to feel numb, "it's fuzzy for some reason, but I had to, I had to, I just had too..." the words coming out of my mouth slowly became more silent, "I just had too."

The floor suddenly seemed to shake under my feet, and my heart squeezed like it were about to crumble. The arms attached to my body were no longer mine as they slumped down, but I did not feel all these things as they happened, for they were overshadowed by the sudden outpour of tears that gushed down my cheeks. Everything that happened rose from the deep pit of fear and worry I had unconsciously been harbouring.

A hand. Her hand. So soft and gentle, came upon my shoulder. She did not speak as my screams of inner pain echoed through the trees, she did not judge either. Her hand, so light I could barely feel it, only sat there as support.

It is said that one can not feel another's pain, yet my unconscious screams that radiated through the air and the sobbing that I had no control over, seemed to seep deeply into the princess's skin. The birds that once sang, stood silently as if in remembrance of the dead, and there were no critters left to be seen in the open.

Only the sound of pain. My pain. My fears and worries fighting each other to get out of my system. Until no more sound could escape from my throat, and yet my jaw lay wide open as if it screamed a silent scream. The tears began to stop only because no liquid was left in my system. Red and runny, my nose seemed to burn.

"Everything's gone," I croaked as my feet gave up under me, "everything, my house, my family, my country, my planet, I'm alone . . . I'm alone. . ."

"You're not alone," the princess replied, sitting down beside me.

"I'm alone . . ."

"I'm with you."

"I'm alone."

"Your not, I'm with you."

"I'm alone." I wailed, my lips trembling as isolation settled in.

"Lana, I haven't left and will never leave you until you are home."

"LIAR," I screeched "WHY ON EARTH WOULD YOU CARE?"

"I told you before, I don't know, but I'll be with you, I will *always* be with you," she said as she pulled me in for a hug, "hear my heartbeat? Focus on it, everything will be alright."

As if I was a dying kitten, her delicate hands gently stroked my hair. Her heartbeat sounded like a calm ocean wave that could put an insomniac to sleep.

"It's ok, everything will be ok," she whispered.

Her heartbeat, echoing through my ears, began to soothe my confused soul. My trembling body began to calm in her presence.

"But you don't know me," I whispered.

"But my soul seems to know yours."

Silence. Our souls entwined. A connection that had no beginning.

"But why?"

"I don't know," she said with a smile.

Chapter 10

    The banquet hall re-welcomed us with the smell of different sizzling meats of which I could not identify. The long table, brimming with different grains and vegetables, let loose steam that seemed to beckon us over.

    "Do you not have a family?" I asked, rather confused as to why Ashta was the only royal person I had seen.

    "Mhm," she replied as she sat down at the foot of the table.

    "Where are they?"

    "I don't know."

    I didn't pursue the matter further, for who am I to pry on such delicate topics?

    "This is grade b ins," said the princess as a servant, with long pointy ears, placed a slice of meat onto my plate.

    "What is it?"

    "A type of livestock, I assume you have livestock where you are from?"

    "We do but no animal called an ins. What does the grade mean?"

    "It's just the quality, grade B is the highest quality you can get,"

    "And grade A?" I asked.

    "That's incredibly rare, barely existent even. I've only ever seen one, but I believe I found a way to increase their number."

    The meat was nothing like I had ever tasted before. Perhaps most similar to veal but with a hint of a different taste that I can not properly describe, sort of like an earthy, sweet flavour. In more simple terms, it tasted like a giant supernatural hug that douses you with an endless supply of endorphins and serotonin.

    "Ashta, this is unworldly,"

    "You don't like it?" She asked.

"Are you kidding, this ins thing whatever it is, is incredible. We have nothing like this at home."

"Oh, I didn't think you'd like it."

"Are you mad? This is. . ." I waved my hands trying to grasp the right word "UNWORLDLY."

She chuckled. Her dazzling smile, showing off her teeth, enhanced how unnaturally pale she was.

"Tomorrow we shall visit the royal library to begin our search." She solemnly declared.

"Should we not visit the place you found me first?" I asked in confusion.

"Well it would be better, but I believe your state of mind is more important, so let's push it off for now," her kind smile showed no sign of judgment only compassion.

I didn't say anything. I was weak and stupid, becoming a hysterical mess was pure proof of that. How could I have lost my senses? I had never felt such a crushing feeling nor had I ever shown my emotions in such a way. I wanted to say it was fine and that we could go back to where she found me, but my beating heart and trembling hands warned of a worst outburst if that were to happen. I smiled, trying to hide the ever growing fear growing inside of me.

Ins. Ins was all I wanted to focus on.

Looking up from my finished plate, the princess sat in perfect serenity watching me. "What?" I smiled.

"You eat far too slow," She replied, her eyebrow lifted accompanied by a witty grin.

"We *barely* started eating,"

"It's been 40 minutes,"

"No?! It's only been 15 minutes,"

"That ins sure played with your head," she laughed as she got up, "let's go you turtle."

<u>Chapter 11</u>

"……therefore parallel universes are impossible," the princess raised her head from the giant book that lay before her, "what do you think?"

"I think I'm bored," I replied, banging my head on the table.

"Lana, this is a serious matter," she sighed.

"Ok ok, but I don't know, Are there any books here about supernatural trees?"

No wall lay empty in the royal library adorned with raw oak shelves which held both the solemn books and unnaturally vibrant plants. If not for the few lit candles, all would be dark.

Drip, drip, drip. I put my finger against the melted wax and watched it dry into a hard case. Warmth introduced itself to my finger.

I got up and gazed at the books. Step after step, my eyes roamed aimlessly as if hoping for a miracle. The air was crisp against my skin as if winter was about to enter the room.

"Lana,"

"Yes?"

"Have you found anything?"

"No, it's cold."

The princess turned around, "your cold?"

I nodded, making my way to the unlit fireplace, "can I?"

She smiled and went back to her book.

After messing about with the logs, I somehow lit a fire, a measly fire, but its little streams of flames quickly started to fill me back with life. In the eminent silence, only the sounds of the soothing crackles of my fire and the occasional rustling of Ashta's book could be heard.

A certain book title caught my eye **The history of fables and myths**. I grabbed it and went back to the fireplace.

The cover was sturdy yet showed signs of age. Dust flew into the air as I opened a random page, they danced away as if relieved to finally be free. The page was soft and seemed as if it had been soaked by the sun. Underlined at the top of the page, the word '**Dinosaurs**' revealed the content of the chapter.

"Ashta,"

"Mhm,"

"What do you know about dinosaurs?"

"Don't tell me you believe in that nonsense," she snorted.

"What?"

She turned around to look at me, "what are you talking about?"

"This book says dinosaurs are a myth."

"And?"

"But they're not."

"What?" The princess jumped out of her seat and made her way beside me.

"Dinosaurs are extinct but not a myth," I explained.

"So you've seen a dinosaur before?" She asked in utter shock.

"No," I laughed, "they died before humans existed."

"so they are a myth?"

"No, there are skeletons and fossils strewn all around the world."

"Have you ever seen one though?" She asked unconvinced.

"Ya, plenty."

"That doesn't make sense," she sighed and picked the book off my lap.

"What are you doing?" I asked.

"Looking at the table of contents," she muttered, then flicked through the pages, "look at this."

A large picture of a narwhal occupied half the page.

"What about this?" Ashta gaped at me.

"A narwhal?"

"Are they extinct where you are from too?"

"No, they're still alive."

"What?" Utter astonishment filled up in her eyes, "SERIOUSLY?"

"Mhmm" I nodded.

"If we go to your world, can I take one with me?" She asked in amazement.

"Uhh, If you're able to get your hands on one I guess?"

"THEN WE MUST FIND YOUR WORLD FAST,' she declared.

My head rolled back with laughter "for a narwhal?"

"YES, A NARWHAL, DO YOU KNOW WHAT THIS MEANS, WE'LL BE LEGENDS. THE PRINCESS WHO OWNS A NARWHAL. A REAL NARWHAL!" She jumped up and down.

"You're making this sound like you found out unicorns exist." I choked, trying to hold in the tears of laughter.

She stopped jumping.

"What?" I asked in a sudden serious tone.

"You're telling me you have narwhals but not unicorns?"

"What?" It was my turn to be confused, "unicorns exist here?" I slowly asked.

"Yeah?"

"No..."

"Yes."

"No."

"They do."

"OH MY GOSH," I could hardly breathe, and my eyes slowly welled up.

We both doubled over with laughter as if little schoolgirls, the solemn air filled with euphoria. Shaking and trembling, tears streaming down our faces. Hearing ourselves only have the ability to squeak and screech, made our stomachs clench with pain.

"I – I – I – I c———can't breath," ashta chocked.

"U- U – Unicorns" I replied, and again we fell to the floor.

****

"Are narwhals dangerous?" Ashta asked after we had calmed down.

"I don't know, they're animals," I asked, my arms cushioning my head.

"Yeah but, you know how unicorns crave murder?"

"They what?" I sat up.

"Yeah, so I was wondering if narwhals were the same because I don't think I would want a murderous animal."

"I beg your pardon?"

She looked up at me "so?"

"Unicorns aren't fluffy lovable creatures?"

"No," she shuddered.

"But their magical horn?"

"Uh, magical?"

"Mhm."

"Well, they use it to kill their prey, and magic isn't real here unless you count their blood's healing abilities."

"Can they talk?"

"No."

"Then how do you know they crave murder?"

"Mind readers."

I sighed, not surprised by this new revelation.

"Do you think there may be some myth about my world or something?" I said, sitting up.

I grabbed the book laid on the floor, still opened on the page with the giant narwhal. I chuckled as I skimmed through the pages, the narwhal still in my mind.

The land of humans

"Ashta look at this."

"Let me see," she said as she snatched the book "the land of humans?"

"Don't snatch, let me read," I replied taking the book back, "the land of humans, a fictional planet that can be found in many classical works. What has made this myth survive the generations is all thanks to the unique representation of humans. In this land, humans are the rulers and are intelligent beings…. What?"

"Let me see," Astra replied pulling the book from me once more, "how strange, perhaps it's a mistake?"

"What, how?"

"Maybe they were going to say the *only* intelligent beings?"

"I guess but still…."

"Go look for more myth books and I'll try to understand this." Ashta smiled.

I got up and faced the books again. The books of which I started to hate. The books of which existed too many for me to read all. The books. The books.

"The books…"

"Hm?" Said Ashta

"Isn't there a book catalogue or something?"

"No idea, no one really comes here."

I sighed.

Chapter 12

I did not sleep that night. Thoughts endlessly flowed through my mind. The humans are intelligent beings? Obviously, some sort of mistake, and yet something felt off.

I got out of bed and made my way to the giant window. The moon, the one thing that felt normal. If only it could give me its serenity, its peace. *Perhaps, it's not too bad here? Why do I even want to go home?* I sighed. I felt like I was losing my mind. Perhaps I was.

I reluctantly picked up one of the books I had taken with me and skimmed through it. Nothing. Nothing new, nothing important.

"Why?" I whispered to the sleeping walls "why me?"

They did not reply. I lifted my head up, resting it on the wall. The moon smiled a sorry smile. I smiled back.

"Why? oh eternal moon, how am I even here?"

No reply.

I smiled, *perhaps it's not too bad here. Perhaps...*

Sleep engulfed me as if the moon herself had heard my cries.

****

She was so pretty. Is pretty? Who is she? A deer. So pretty.

"Hello, deer, you're so pretty," I said in a wispy voice that didn't sound like it belonged to me.

Pretty deer. With... with... with.... bleeding eyes?

"Are you hungry darling?" It whispered.

"But your eyes..."

Everything was murky, dancing strangely in a haze. *Is this fog? Pretty deer.... Bloody eyes.*

"Are you hungry?" It repeated, red dripping down its face.

"Yes?" I slurred.

"Well then it is simple, do not eat."

A bunch of gurgling sounds that carried no meaning come out of my mouth. Pools of blood dripped around the deer's feet. Blood. Blood. Drip. Drip…. Then all was dark until it was not. For the moon seemed to be waiting. Waiting for what?

What was that haze? Perhaps a dream, but the bloody eyes. *Was it the same one I saw in the forest?* "Do not eat" echoed in my ears. Something hung in the air, neither good nor evil, if there even is a difference.

The book still lay on my lap. It contained nothing on deers. Skimming through, my eyes caught sight of huge red eyes on the wrinkled yellow page.

The Legend of the dying eyes

The eyes that have seen unexplainable trauma can only run away from it. However, if it runs away suffering will only follow. Those of the dying eyes are tortured with the sight of agony and torture, the more it has seen the more it will cry tears of blood, the blood of those in pain. Some say those of the dying eyes eventually wither away from extreme distress, others say they are on a never ending journey to lessen their misery. How? By stopping a torturous fate.

The moon began to disappear getting ready for the sun to take its place. No point in sleeping now, not that there was a drop of sleep in me. I got up placing the book aside. *What now?* Nothing. Frustration echoed through me as my mind flowed with empty thoughts.

What to believe? What not to believe? The dying eyes, a torturous fate. I saw those eyes, technically twice if we consider dreams as reality, and why would they not be? What makes dreams unreal? What makes our awake life real? Our world contains such strange concepts that seem to go unquestioned, but I should focus on the more important matters.

Torturous fate? Was it my fate that was torturous? Perhaps it was the giant spider's fate, yet there was no spider in my dream. Although, I didn't know if I should believe in my dream, it could have been merely a dream, as in a made up vision my unconscious brain made, but so could the whole of reality.

"Arghhh" I groaned out loud.

Such unnecessary thoughts plagued my mind. *Who cares if life is real or not?! Who cares if dreams are reality?! Must I think of such a ridiculous concept?!* I have no control over these things, no power to change, yet I endlessly torture myself with such ridiculous thoughts. I was tired. I am tired. If only there was a switch that could turn your brain off. If only life was that simple. I just wanted to know if the deer was trying to save my fate or the spiders! Not to question reality itself!

I banged my head against the wall. Again and again. It hurt. I needed to feel something and yet I've been feeling too much recently. It hurts inside. In my heart, in my soul. Pain should be felt outside through pain receptors, so why did it feel like something inside of me was fighting to breathe under a mass of water? Something weighing it down. Weighing what? I do not know. Perhaps my soul, perhaps my heart. I dislike using the word my in this context, it feels too personal. Too personal. As if I am real. *I do not want to be real.*

Chapter 13

I flinched, startled by the sound of rustling. The red eyes gleamed at me from the book that was still open in my lap. I fell asleep. Good, some moments of peace, even if I don't remember it.

Creak. A slow scratching sound buzzed through the air. My head immediately swung to the door.

"Hello?" I spoke to the air.

A small head popped from the barely ajar door, right under where my vision originally was looking, waiting for someone to enter.

"Hello." A little squeak returned my greeting.

A small girl, no older than 9, peered through the door. Her blue eyes, so light it could be mistaken for the sky, widened in curiosity, with her long pointy ears like swords sticking out of her flowy golden brown hair. An elf, I thought, an elf child.

Her soft thin lips slightly parted as if wanting to say something but immediately closed like it was merely her third eye needing to blink. Such a funny thing blinking is.

"May I help you?" I asked.

Her head tilted slightly more, "can I touch your hair?"

"What?"

"Your hair," she squeaked.

I did not reply. One, because too many questions wanted to bombard out of my mouth, and two, because she came running in anyways.

Such an agile little creature. One second, her eyes beamed at the door, the next, she was standing in front of me. Even my poofy hair seemed to be in utter confusion as the little thing poked and prodded between the tangles.

"Uh excuse me?" I said as I stood up.

"I've only ever seen one," she said nonchalantly.

"One what?"

"I tried to go play with them, but mother says it's too dangerous blah blah blah." She rolled her eyes.

"Who the hell are you?" I questioned in bewilderment, swiping away the eye crust that somehow builds up when you're asleep.

"Hmm? I'm Alleta." She replied as if it was the most obvious thing in the world.

"And?"

"Can I touch your hair again?"

"I beg your pardon?"

"I've never touched a human!"

"What?"

"Pleaseeeeee."

"What are you even doing here?" I said as my eyebrows furrowed further than they already were.

"Ugh, Princess Ashta told me to get you," she rolled her eyes, "can I touch your hair now?"

"Ashta?" I asked, "Child speak in full sentences, I have no idea what on earth you're going on about."

"I am not a child, I am 8."

"Ok?"

"So that means I'm not a child, now please lower your head." She smiled, her eyes wide enough to fall out of their sockets.

Children. Such unnecessarily necessary creatures. Creatures which swim in curiosity and innocence then are crushed by our lovely reality. *I don't dislike children*, I thought as I leaned my head slightly for her to reach my hair.

"It's so coooool," she giggled as she pulled on a strand and watched it bounce back into place, "it's like a slinky!"

Well, that's one thing our world has in common. Slinkies.

"Thanks, I guess?" I replied.

"I can't hold Miss shams's hair long enough to make it bounce."

"Uh Why?"

"She's a fire dima." She looked at me as if I were the child, and an incompetent one at that.

"Oh ok that's cool, so Ashta sent you?" I asked hoping to finish the conversation.

"I like your hair more than Miss. Shams."

I took a deep breath. Children, the epitome of annoyance. "I don't know who that is, so just tell me what Ashta wants."

"Yes you doooo," she sang, "she told me she's cleaned your roooooom."

She was talking about Maple. *Shams, so that's what her name was. Fire dima? That made sense. I knew something was off with her hair.*

"Ok, that's lovely what does ashta want."

"She wants you to come for breakfast," She finally replied, "she was going to send Miss. Akhthar but I knew that this may be the only time I can touch a human."

"Uh what," I shook my head wanting to laugh but who has the energy for such things when they first wake up?

"Well, I-"

"I'm too tired," I cut her off, "let's just go to ashta."

"Okiessss," she sang as she skipped towards the door.

Here we go, the start of another day, perhaps the last day. The last day I'm here or the last day of reality? Who cares, I wanted breakfast, not a headache.

****

"Uh, so who are you exactly?" I asked as we strolled through the magnificent hallways.

"Alleta."

"So your Ashta's sister?"

She snorted "do I look like ashta's sister?"

"Uh yeah?"

I mean sure her skin didn't resemble a transparent ice shard but she was pale too. Her eyes may not have been a striking purple but they were strikingly blue. Well, the ears did kind of throw everything off but if she's not her sister who on earth was she? What other child would have access to a palace?

She rolled her eyes. Too much sass for such a small thing. As she bounced from foot to foot, her hair swished behind her. The golden light from the windows lit her up as she walked past them, making her hair switch from golden silk to a waterfall of lightly roasted almonds.

I then noticed that the floor felt incredibly soft, as I look down I realize I forgot to wear shoes again. *I mean, the palace has carpets for a reason don't they?* Although, their reason is probably not for the comfort of some random lost girl. Either way, I'm not bothered to go back.

Step after step, my feet sank through the plush carpet, the ceilings towering above us. "Do you guys not have golf carts or something?" I asked.

"Golf carts in a palace?" She looked at me as if I had gone mad.

"So everyone just walks around everywhere?"

"Yeah."

If royalty can do anything, summon anything, why not use that power for fun? I like to think that if I were royalty, I'd have slides instead of stairs and chocolate fountains spotted around the place. A little spot to boost dopamine. Or an even better idea, each fountain could contain different delicacies. One could be milk chocolate, one could be dark, one can even be of milk!

Ah, to be drowned in the ocean of such smells! To have the sky rain down whatever the stomach craves! A pantomime of sweetness traveling through your nose, a marching band of flavours parading their way to the lungs!

Thousands of oxygen masks hanging in a room, each holding within a blast of aromas, and a button to demand the possessor to be shown! Ah, let it rain! Let it rain whatever the heart desires!

A library of packaged goodness! Shelves upon shelves of indescribable confections! Seemingly infinite selections, a place where the unimaginable exists!

To run between such fumes, shower in its delight, kidnap what is theirs and make it only mine! Share it with the others, let them see what can only be breathed, let the smell cascade down their throats, show them the miracle of taste!

Ah but what if the stomach craves the wrong? What if the stomach demands the evil!? Then the land of delights becomes a land of regret. A land of addiction! A place of darkness and horrors, the truth of the individual!

Restriction. It's a funny thing that plays with mind. One deeply craves what one cannot have. I wonder whether certain things are truly amazing, addicting even, or merely an inaccurate representation from being restricted. Human meat is said to be delicious, addicting, but is it truly addicting? Truly amazing? Or is the idea addicting and amazing because of said restriction? Why am I using human meat as an example?

"Ta daaaa!"

"What?" I jumped.

"We have arrivedddd," squealed Alleta.

Oh right. Breakfast.

<u>Chapter 19</u>

Honey. I could smell honey, "freshly picked." Said Ashta.

"Picked?" I asked, confused about the lexical choice.

"Well, what word do you use when gathering honey?"

"Um, I don't know maybe harvest?"

"Eh, harvest is more befitting of cattle right."

Perhaps not all lexical choices carry the same connotations here.

Sweet. The smell. Like a dream floating through the abyss. Fresh cotton and honey harmonised in the air like how I imagine it would on the first day of summer. The weather too, a warmth that felt cooling in comparison to the warmth of my blood. A sense of calmness like a warm bath, or perhaps the quiet before the storm. *Stop being a pessimist*, I thought to myself.

"Nothing like honey on warm toast," said Ashta.

"Mhm"

The thick liquid oozed over my lips, sticky yet refreshing. Pessimism. Pessimism. *I've never been a big fan of honey.* Pessimism. *What am I if not a pessimist?* The toast, the sweet goop swam in my mouth. Honey. Sweet sweet pessimism.

"...got it?"

"Mhm?" Someone replied to Ashta.

It was me. I replied to Ashta. But who am I? What am I In a world such as this? A pessimist? *My brain hurts, but that's nothing new.* I am Lana, but who is Lana? Or perhaps, *what* is Lana?

"Are you ok Lana?"

"Yeah," she replied, or maybe it was me.

I was lost in a nonexistent cloud, an infinite fog that danced away in my brain. I was losing my sanity. I *am* losing my sanity. Although, what is sanity? And how do we know we are sane in the first place? Perhaps I'm gaining sanity. Though that sounds like something an insane person would say.

"Your tea is going to get cold you know."

"What?" And just like that, I had snapped back to reality.

"Your tea."

"Oh right, what is it?"

"Lavender I think," Ashta replied.

An elegant cup and saucer sat in front of me. How did I not notice it? Painted on it were delicate purple flowers, pastel like the sunset. Swirling on vines with dainty little leaves by their sides. The tea itself was also a magnificent sight. A transparent pastel purple.

I raised the cup to my lips and watched the tea form elegant little waves. My eyes filled with the serenity of lavender fields as I took the first sip. Slightly cold yet wondrous.

"Where's my toast?" I asked looking around for what I remembered to be in front of me.

"You ate it while you were in la la land," laughed Ashta, "you want another one?"

'No, I'm not hungry," I replied

Of course I wasn't hungry, I must have devoured an army of toast while I was going through what I can only call a psychotic breakdown.

"Ok so basically I have two ideas," Started Ashta.

"Mhm."

"We can either go to the public library or..." she paused and looked up at me.

"Or?"

"I don't know what to call the place, it's a bit eh," She shrugged.

"What's that supposed to mean?"

"It's a bit underground you could say."

"Underground?" My eyebrows raised in confusion.

"Yeah," she replied as I shook my head in a way that asked for a better explanation.

"Well," she sighed "it's not really supposed to exist."

"So it's illegal?"

"No, well maybe, actually no, the place is, but not the place *place*."

"What on earth are you talking about?"

"It's a market that's technically illegal but not really."

"A black market?"

"No, that's illegal, this is kind of legal, you know what? The logistics don't matter that much."

"Right..." I replied sarcastically as I got up to follow Ashta.

We made our way out of the dining room and walked down the endless halls until we reached an extravagant arched wooden door. The entrance. Or the exit depending on which way you look at it.

It towered above us, a door fit for a giant. *Perhaps that's why it's so big, perhaps they have giants here who visit.* Glad that my psychotic musings had finally taken a whimsical turn, I smiled at the thought. Delicate ashta, as pale and fragile as a snowflake, having tea with a giant creature squished in a giant chair that is still too small for it. I would pay to see that.

To the side of the door hung a couple of coats, no, they were cloaks. How stereotypical for such a place like this, yet how delighted was I to see them! A cloak, the epitome of a fantasy story, I would finally live every reader's dream. "Will we ride horses?" My eyes lit up at the thought.

"Uh, what?"

"Horses..." I repeated.

"We're going by car..." Ashta said as she looked at me like I was insane.

"Oh."

The world wasn't as stereotypical as I thought it was. Gutted is the only word I can use to describe what I felt.

"Do you know what a car is?" Ashta asked as she handed me a cloak.

"What?"

"A car?"

"Of course, I know what a car is."

"Oh ok."

"I thought since you guys have cloaks then you'd have horses too."

"What?"

"You know what, never mind."

"We can go by horse if you want to though."

"Won't we look weird?"

"Not really, a lot of people still use horses here."

So I was right! At least slightly, "yess let's ride horsessssss!" I jumped up and down, the cloak that I now was wearing swam behind me fluidly.

Horses and cloaks! Horses and cloaks! Horses and cloaks! Ah such an opportunity left me ecstatic! Actually, ecstatic would be an understatement, the very discs in my spine could barely manage absorbing the excitement that ran through my back.

Walking up to the door, Ashta banged her fists three times on its wooden frame then knocked in a rhythmic pattern. 1 2.. 1 2.. 1 2.. 1 2 3 4. I wonder what that means. Probably a safety measure.

Creaking slowly, the heavy door started to open. Two men stood wearing deep purple cloaks, their eyes glistening beneath the hood, like a wolf about to pounce. They nodded their heads at Ashta "the car awaits you, your highness," the one on the left grunted.

"No need, get two horses ready please," she replied in a strange manner, stern but elegant, as you'd imagine royalty would.

"That will take an extra fifteen minutes your highness, is that ok?" He grunted again, his gleaming eyes staring into the abyss.

"No problem, we're going to walk, bring them to the gate."

He grunted once more and moved to the side of the door as his companion went the opposite direction so they faced each other.

As we walked past I raised my head to take a peak from underneath my hood, they seemed much taller and muscular. Rough looking, their eyes whispered warnings, make a mistake and your bones will be crushed with a simple flick. Obviously, they did not actually say that, eyes do not verbally talk.

Our feet grazed the stone path beneath us, it's hardness felt unnatural after walking on mostly softer surfaces. The sun was high in the sky yet there was a chill in the air, my breath twirled into wispy puffs floating out of me as if I was a smoke breathing dragon.

The path was lined with dark leaved bushes shaped into neat cubes. Beneath them swayed rows of lavender, sending its scent swimming between the waves of chilly breeze. Pastel pink flowers also mixed in between the lavender, their petals puffy almost fluffy even, as if they were a bunch of feathers.

"It's cold," I said as I hugged my cloak pulling it closer to my shivering body.

"Oh? I guess it is getting less warm these days," Ashta replied unfazed, "would you like to return?"

Yes, though not because of the cold, to continue was an act of danger. To continue was to leave the safety that wasn't even meant for me, if safety even existed at all. For who is truly safe when a single thought could be the end of one's life? A small lump formed in my throat as I suppressed the urge to fall into the depths of depletion.

"No," I said reluctantly as I looked back to the castle slowly getting smaller behind us.

It was stunning. Grey yet bold among the dark trees and bushes. Tall towers loomed beneath the clouds with triangular tops, a part of me looked for cascading hair falling out of one of the windows, thankfully there was not. The castle perfectly stood as if conjured from a world that does not exist except in the mind.

Does something not exist if it exists in the mind? Do the creations of the brain not count as real? It should, should it not? It can not be said that existence is defined by having physical attributes otherwise would that not mean love does not exist? What about hate? Sadness? Why are the worlds I have created in my head considered fake? It's non-existing but it exists in the head, that should be enough. If feelings are real then shouldn't the worlds in my brain exist too? What makes existence in our reality different than existence of the minds reality?

"Lana," Interrupted Ashta.

"Yes?" I replied.

"Have you ever tried lavender cake?"

"What, umm no," I smiled at the random question.

"I love lavender and it tastes divine when mixed with sugar."

"What if you were to *mix* reality with what is created in the mind?" I thought out loud

"I beg your pardon?" She replied in bewilderment.

"Would that be insanity?"

"Insanity is you right now," she laughed.

"Perhaps, perhaps I am."

"Your perfectly sane Lana," she frowned slightly.

"No, do you not feel... feel like there's something we're missing?" I asked.

"In finding your homes?"

"No," I sighed "something more, something deeper, something just ever so slightly out of reach. Ah if I can just grab the very edge I'd be able to pull it in!"

"Sometimes," she whispered.

"Hm?"

"Sometimes," her voice floated alongside the cold air, "but... what if it's not a soft blanket but rather a giant boulder?"

"You understand what I'm saying?" I asked in surprise never having experienced someone grasp the thoughts that hide behind my words.

"What if that thing is out of reach because it would crush us whole?" She continued, perhaps having not heard my question.

"And turn us into a mess of bloodied consciousness." I continued.

"Mhm," she nodded sadly. "Perhaps it's better for the edge to forever be out of reach."

"But wouldn't the tragic end be worth the answer?"

She did not answer. Leaving the air to drown in the thoughts alone.

The gate began to loom in front of us. Two different cloak men stood waiting, each of their hands twirled with leather reins connected to our ride. Why am I calling them cloak men? Are they guards? Who cares, I want to call them cloak men.

The cloak men nodded their heads, their faces as hard as stone, as the horses awaited us beside them. One as if submerged in the depths of the night sky, its coat gleaming as if devouring the light that dared pass by. The other purely white, not a shadow could possibly dull such a lustrous complexion.

"I'll take the white one," said Ashta as she effortlessly threw herself on, "come on Lana."

I walked up to the black horse that seemed to grow larger the closer I got to it and threw my leg into the stirrup. Heaving my body up, I magnificently threw my other leg and sat perfectly straight on the horse. Or so I wish. What actually happened was quite interesting to say the least, I actually think I saw one of the cloak men stifle a laugh as my foot thrashed towards the sky.

"Lana, what on earth are you doing?!" Ashta barked.

"Getting on?"

"Do you know how to ride a horse?"

"Yeah, I took lessons when I was younger for a month," I assured as I wiggled my upside down head trying to haul myself the right way up.

"And that's how they taught you to mount a horse?" She said sarcastically.

"I just need to brush up my riding skills that's all."

"Rightttt," Ashta laughed as she jumped off her horse, "ok I'll help," she flipped me up so I was back to standing one foot on the stirrup and held me as I somehow managed to get my other leg to the other side, "there we go, was that so hard?" She chuckled, jumping back onto her horse, more elegantly than the first time might I add.

I ran my hands through the horse's mane, sinking my fingers between its raven locks. My fingers twirled through the rough strands that seemed to withhold a softness that could not be physically touched. It shook its head as if in delight or perhaps in disgust as I selfishly sat on top of it. What was I supposed to do? Ask the horse for consent?

"Open the gates," Ashta ordered, as she clicked her tongue for the horse to move.

I mimicked her clicks in hopes of salvaging my horse riding reputation, but of course, it did not budge, "um Ashta?" I called.

"Yeah?" She said looking back at me.

"It won't move."

"Click your tongue."

"I did," I replied then started to click away my tongue again.

"Hit its side with the heels of your feet."

"It's not working," I declared as I tapped my feet.

"Harder," she commanded.

"I don't want to hurt it."

"It doesn't hurt it."

I took a deep breath and slammed my heels. It did not budge. "It's not working Ashta."

She took a deep breath and jumped off her horse "fine let's swap," she replied then helped me off my own, "if I were you I'd go demand a refund for those so called horse lessons," she grinned.

I rolled my eyes as she pushed me up the white horse, "your horses are just weird."

"Sure definitely, it's totally the horse's fault." She laughed jumping on the black horse.

I don't know what superpowers she has but one click of her tongue and that stupid horse began to move, "how on earth?!"

"Maybe it doesn't like you," she laughed.

I rolled my eyes and clicked my own tongue, thankfully the white horse seemed to like me as it started to move.

Chapter 20

Once we left the premises of the castle we rode down a slope, through trees and flowers that one cannot describe but as the descendants of beauty. Withholding a distinct calmness within the very air it floats, shrouded by a soft wind carrying the delicate smell of freedom.

The long grass tickled the horse's hoofs, the occasional long strands brushing my own feet. A slight brush nothing more, nothing less, as if a few strands had built up the courage to examine us, the outsiders, then returning to share its discoveries amongst its fellows. They leaned against each other, whispering rumours of our comings, "what is that!"

"The forbidden creatures!"

"Don't move!"

"Please, have mercy!" or perhaps they were merely dancing to the music of the wind, unaware of our very existence.

How nice it must be to be veiled by a darkened cloud. To live unaware. To not see life nor death. Oh but it is too late for me! For who can gouge their eyes out after being able to see? But to have the chance to unlock those chains! To forget the world, no to forget existence! To just be. To glisten like the raindrops that moisten the grass, sliding slowly down its shimmering green facade. To swap places with the soft air that drowns in my lungs, the soft air that entwines my soul as the sound of distant leaves crunch amongst themselves. Oh how lovely it would all be! A mind of bliss, filled with nothing but roaming clouds. A meadow of nothingness, no future, no present, no past!

Surrounded by the scuttles of some small animals and the melodies of the birds, we marched with the flowing wind. It took quite a while to get to the bottom.

"Keep your head down and don't take off your hood," Said Ashta her purple eyes glowing beneath her own hood.

"Why?" I asked.

"We don't want to be noticed."

"Why?"

"Do you only ask why?" She rolled her eyes.

"Well, you only give half answers." I huffed.

"Well the place we're going to doesn't usually have royalty running around, so we don't want anyone to notice us," the village began to loom in front of us, nestled between two mountains. "Leave the talking to me ok?"

The buildings began to grow as we got closer, little round wooden huts with two or three smaller circle structures on top, like a wedding cake almost. Excitement ruffled through me accompanied by curiosity as I noticed how each floor's roof stuck out similar to a bucket hat. Yes, that's the perfect way to describe the structure, two or three bucket hats stacked onto each other. With elongated oval doors and circular windows, incredibly beautiful and nothing like I had ever seen, scattered around randomly minding nature's path.

In between the houses was a lake with a path that seemed to float on top of it, a bridge. The horse's shoes clanged on the wood as it began to walk on it. Looking to the left and right, I marveled at my surroundings.

"How do they get up there?" I asked Ashta as I pointed to the doors nestled into the mountain.

"Paths, wings, animals, depends on them," she shrugged.

Further along, a child like creature swam in the lake as a lady, perhaps his mother, sat on a chair in front of their hut.

"Keep your head down Lana," Whispered Ashta.

"Good morning," sang a voice, the lady.

"Good morning," replied Ashta.

As curiosity got the better of me, I took a quick peek at the child. Doe eyed and incredibly skinny, his arms and legs were longer than the rest of his body's proportions. He splashed his lanky body around but what caught my eyes was his hair, or more specifically what was on top of it. Sturdy atop his head sat antlers. His brown curls hid the base making it hard to distinguish wether they were real or not, though by the way they held themselves it was quite obvious that they were no mimics.

My eyes moved to his strangely long fingers, little droplets splashed down from them almost like a slide lacking a curve. His every movement seemed so profound though I can not say wether that was because of what he was or if it was merely because he was a child. His neck protruded from his shoulders like a tree from the ground, exhibiting his average sized head that carried his strangely huge eyes. Deep brown eyes, almost gold.

I wished I could look at the women too but that would be far too risky, I would have had to raise my head quite a bit.

"What is that?" I whispered to Ashta as we moved past.

"A child?" She whispered back confused.

"No I mean what is the child, is it a dima?"

"Oh, no he's an elka."

"What does that mean?"

With a giant sigh she whispered back, "elka's, intelligent beings, they have antlers, big eyes, and long proportions. Though they seem skinny they are not, it's just their long proportions giving that illusion, they are, in fact, very strong," and then continued with an almost mutter "I find it funny when people underestimate them…"

The further we went the more huts and beings began to appear. A pack of winged children raced by, approximately around the ages of 7 and 8, one pushing her friend with her bold red and blue wings, while a third scurried past them as they were distracted. A fourth lugged along, her relaxed wing, a stunning shade of sage green, trailing behind her on the grass. She made little huffs that feathered her wings, as if saying she was tired and had had enough.

"What is-"

"Shh" shushed Ashta.

Another child came up to them with an innocent smile, his head filled with protruding snakes sharing the opposite of his expression. A few smaller snakes also protruded from his little face, one on his left cheek, two on the right side of his forehead, and another singular one on the right side of his jaw. They slithered through the air, showing off their gradient scales, beginning at the base with red and gradually transitioning to orange with the upper sides of their scales a solid ocean blue. Their tongues flicking in and out almost as if to get a better understanding of the winged children.

The green winged girl seemed to gain a bounce in her step as he began to skip alongside her. Who knows what raced in between their heads, or if what raced even was understood by either one as they blabbered, unfortunately for my nosy self, too far away for me to catch any words.

As we continued, a toddler with neon green hair appeared walking along the stream, his nose deep in the clutches of a flower. He continued to waddle along besides what seemed to be his father who shared the same vibrant locks. A green so unnaturally bright it almost hurt the eyes to look at and yet my eyes seemed to refuse to let go of the sight.

Further along, a teenager sat beneath a tree reading a book as she sat on what looked like a small fuzzy bean bag but was actually her long hair made up of what seemed to be wool, sheep's wool. Thick and long, the cream coloured curls flew all over the place, so large it almost hide her face. It sat in a beautiful cozy frizz as if they were a barrier against the outer world, not even letting her feet touch the grass beneath her.

They lived normally yet looked starkly different. Of course, they lived normally, why wouldn't they? For some reason I had excepted something else, I'm not sure what but it wasn't normal. At least not my normal.

"Stop staring." Whispered Ashta.

"Hm? Oh, right sorry."

How can one not look at such peculiar spectacles? How can one overcome such urges to know? To understand?

I question such things frequently, what happens when you run behind curiosity? I fear that chasing such ideas, believing in enlightenment will only lock you in a cage, and yet what else is there to do when you are constantly parched for a drop of an answer? So many questions, so many answers. A burning obsession that cannot be suppressed, yet let it be free and it'll incinerate your brain and soul. So much to observe but will I ever understand? *Who, no, what am I?*

A swirling sweetness began to scent the fresh air, something caramelised, making my mouth drool with longing. Alongside it, was the smell of flowers that seemed to reside throughout the whole kingdom, a light airy smell mixed with the fresh cotton that wafted from the clean laundry hanging outside some of the huts.

The sound of the hustles and bustles of life began to beat louder the closer we got to the heart of the town, the smell grew to make me dizzy with hunger. Maybe I should have eaten another piece of toast.

The huts started to scatter further away from the middle and more adults began to appear running errands. Going further along, little shops and stalls advertising different bits and bobs emerged into our eyesight. The caramel smell began to twirl in my heart, the aroma urging me to come to it.

"Ashta," I murmured.

"Yes?" She whispered back without looking at me.

"What's that smell?"

"You mean the nuts?"

"Nuts?

"Yeah, caramelised nuts,"

"Can we get some?" I asked.

"Uh, I don't know Lana we don't really have the time and-"

"Please Ashta it won't take long," I begged.

"Fine fine just keep your voice down." She hushed.

Steering to the side, we stopped in front of a wooden stall harmonising with brown hues. Vibrating beneath the strengthening sun, it gave off the cozy smell of warm caramel, sweet enough to soften the heart of one whom knows only of harshness.

"Mm," grunted a short stout man standing by the cart, boasting his height of a 6 year old child.

"We'll take two please." Said Ashta.

His face hid behind a scruffy beard reaching the lower part of his ribs and wore a fully black and seemingly old outfit with heavy boots. Grunting once more, he wobbled behind the cart.

I have gone my whole entire life laughing at the dramatic depiction of cartoon characters that end up flying when they smell food, but I think I finally understand. As he shoveled the nuts into the cups, the aroma burst with the movement. I won't lie, I drooled a bit. The man did not seem amused.

"That's a fiver," his deep gravelly voice croaked.

Ashta whipped out the royal medallion from underneath her cloak, letting it twinkle under the sun's rays. Giving us the little cups, the man grumbled seemingly dissatisfied.

As he raised his arm to hand the cups, his sleeve rolled down to reveal his arms entwined with bulging strips, almost like a branch had climbed up and embedded itself deep into his very bones. As if snakes had trapped themselves beneath his skin and demanded to be released. The bulges seemed to slither as he moved his arm towards us, meandering atop his veins.

As we rode off, I whispered, "Does the medallion not give us away?"

"Hm? Oh no, anyone can have a medallion," Ashta babbled, her face fully stuffed, "glad we stopped, this reminds me of my childhood."

"Yeah," I replied distractedly as I threw in a nut in my mouth, a jewel of sweetness.

The place was so lively with the chatters of people as we trodded by. What once bothered me now was music to my ears. *Human life!* Well, technically not human but life all the same. A bell rang from who knows where, tumbling its melody through the town. The crackles of life beating away.

A ginger cat slept soundly on a passing fence, who knows perhaps it was as human as I was. Well, not a human, perhaps being is a better word.

Turning sharply to the left, we entered through an alleyway. I doubt I would have noticed it had I not been following Ashta. Trotting behind her, I gazed at the walls that hugged us from either side, as if it were a fox hole. The sun disappearing, left a suffocating darkness behind.

A strange murky smell steamed the sticky air, tingling the tip of my nose. My cloak ruffled ever so slightly as a random gust of wind danced between the two endless walls. The sound of the horse's trots echoed an irksome tune. "Nearly there," whispered Ashta, seeming to be as uncomfortable as I was.

"Nearly there, nearly there, nearly there," The walls whispered back.

Stroking the horse mane to soothe my anxiety, a slight light began to shimmer in front of us. Sounds of life began to return although much quieter than before. "Whatever you do, do not speak," reminded Ashta, the walls once again copied her whispers, echoing the message in case it was not heard.

An oval doorway became present in our sight. Entering it revealed a damp staircase leading downwards, mud tracked all over. I wondered what Ashta planned to do with the horses, but she pushed hers along clanking its feet on the stone steps, beginning to disappear into the unknown as the dim lanterns weakened their sights on her.

Clicking my tongue, my horse began to stumble its way down, tilting me at a worrisome angle. A drip of water trickled on my head, it wasn't raining outside so I'd rather not think of what it was. Drip, drip, drip, sang the echos of the wall as the puddles of water vibrated with each drop. Drip drip drip. Was that the mysterious droplets or the beatings of my speeding heart? It is hard to say, my thoughts weren't at their strongest as I clutched my horse with the strength that seemed to have come from nowhere.

Clip clop clip clop echoed the walls harmonising with the depressing droplets or perhaps the beatings of my heart. Then, the echoes stopped. Flat ground stood beneath and what a relief it felt. Though I could barely see my hands, I wouldn't be surprised if they had turned purple from the death grip.

From afar, I could hear the slight echos of galloping. Clicking my tongue I began again. An endless tunnel. Mind numbing. A question plagued my mind. Why does it all feel like a dream? The walls echoed my heavy breath, *I wasn't made for horse riding.*

A shiver ran down my spine. *What is that feeling called? Is it a feeling? Or am I merely a wandering insanity who feels differently from the rest?* Surreal? Bizarre? No, it's more like drowning in an invisible cloud. *I can breathe, I can see, so I should be fine. Right? I am real. I am me.*

Why do I feel unreal? As if I was merely watching a movie? As if I were a ghost staring at someone who looked like me? *Why do I feel unreal?*

On and on and on I galloped. On and on and on and on and on On and on and on and on and on and on and on and on and on and on and on and on and on on and on

on and on and on and on and on and on and on and on
and on and on and on and on on and on and on and on
and on and on and on on and on and on and on and on
and on and on and on and on and on and on and on and
on and on and on and on on and on and on and on and on
and on and on on and on and on and on and on and on
and on and on and on and on and on and on and on and
on and on and on on and on and on and on and on and on
and on on and on and on and on and on and on and on
and on and on and on and on and on and on and on and
on and on on and on and on and on and on and on and on
on and on and on and on and on and on and on and on
and on and on and on and on and on and on and on and
on on and on and on and on and on and on and on on and
on and on and on and on and on and on and on and on
and on and on and on and on and on and on and on on
and on and on and on and on and on and on and on and
on and on and on and on and on and on and on and on
and on and on and on and on and on and on on and on
and on and on and on and on and on on and on and on
and on and on and on and on and on and on ·and on and
on and on and on and on and on on and on and on
and on and on and on and on and on and on on and on
and on and on and on and on and on on and on and on
and on and on and on and on and on and on and on and
on and on and on and on and on and on and on and on
and on and on and on and on on and on and on and on
and on and on and on and on and on and on and on and
on and on and on and on on and on and on and on
and on and on and on on and on and on and on and on
and on and on and on and on and on and on and on and
on and on and on and on A Pass and Red and on and on and on
and on and on and on and on on and on and on and on
and on and on and on on and on and on and on and on
and on and on and on and on and on and on and on and
on and on and on and on on and on and on and on and on
and on and on and on on and on and on and on and on
and on and on and on and on and on and on and on and

on and on and on on and on and on and on and on and on and on on and on and on and on and on and on and on and on and on and on and on and on and on and on on and on and on and on and on and on and on and on and on on and on and on and on and on and on and on and on and on on and on and on and on and on and on and on and on and on on and on on and on on and on and on and on and on and on and on and on and on and on and on and on and on and on and on...

Will it ever stop? A forever stretching tunnel, but there must be an end. There must be. Did it even have a beginning? Of course it did, the alleyway, the stairs. But was that really what I was asking?

High pitch screech scraped through my ears, but it wasn't real, I think. My hands began to lose their grip as the heat sucked out their moisture. Wet, sticky. *Am I breathing? Who's breathing? Who's inhaling? Exhaling? Who is moving my lungs? I am Lana and I'm alive*, echoed through something, perhaps my mind.

I pulled on the horse's reign, his gallop began to slow. What was the point of going on? Why was I even here? "Lana," a quick whisper stabbed through the air.

"Hmm?"

"Lana, what's taking you so long?" Ashta, her voice soothing like cool water on a burning wound.

"What?" I echoed back.

"Come on Lana, why are you taking ages?"

Her voice slithered gently from the red gleam in front. I looked behind me. I had taken ten steps away from the stairs.

"Ashta," I squeaked.

"Come on Lana."

"Can we just rest? Take a nap?"

"What? Lana are you ok?"

"Yeah," I sighed.

I hate myself.

"Ok, come along then."

I clicked my tongue and moved forwards, each step getting me closer to the burning light. Her pale face glowed as the red shone behind her, the purple ocean in her eyes fighting for the spotlight as the burning ember tried to sneak through.

"Ok, so the people here can be a bit strange, don't talk to anyone, don't stop for anyone, stay beside me. Alright?"

" Mhm," I nodded.

A coolness clamped onto my hand as if I had dipped them into the heart of the Antarctic. A soft air flew from her gentle hand that squeezed my sweaty palm.

"It'll be alright Lana, I promise."

Her eyes spoke words that could not be said. Gentleness and care that should not exist. Her little smile assuring, whispered that everything will be ok. That I am real, that she's real.

I took a deep breath and nodded, "ok let's go."

Chapter 21

We entered through the arched doorway, well, it was more like a crack in the wall.

My manic eyes rioted against what was presented in front of me. A dim hall of depressed bricks, seemingly with an infinite height, with more cracks lining the wall from top to bottom. Stacks on stacks of holes though each slightly different from the other.

Some lay bare, some with doors, some with fancy signs but a particular hole caught my attention. Stationed two meters off the ground and exhibiting no obvious way to get in, the crack was closed off with a giant bolder, protruding its body half way out of the wall, showing no signs of existence if not for the open sign that laid on it. My mind travelled the depths of my brain to reach a viable conclusion as to how such a door would be opened without the boulder smashing to the ground but alas, no conclusion was ever made.

The crack beneath it housed a much more civil door though still bizarre when compared to a normal one. Pillars of grey metal stretched like the shape of the letter P, a thin door with a random circle to its top right. Upon its facade sat specks of white as if they were moths lazily asleep, unaware of the peculiarity of what they lay on.

A gloopy substance drooled on the walls, slightly red from the lanterns that perched between the doors, or that is what I hoped was the reason for the colour.

A disgustingly green lake ran in the middle, the sides hauntingly red as the gloop on the walls. Drops pattering with the speed of my own racing heartbeat.

A stench lurked in the heavy air making my eyes tear, or perhaps that was the result of the dread that was slowly pulling me with its arms of trepidation. Sewers. We had entered the sewers.

I turned wide eyed towards Ashta who, next to me, was pulling her hood lower. She glared into the depths of my soul. *Not a word must escape my mouth but the sewers?!*

Potentially my last hope, my salvation, hidden in the rotting depths of this world. My ears rang as the thoughts of failure suffocated me. Fear himself seemed to have manifested in front of my eyes, dancing to the beat of my racing heart, slowly coming closer without particularly taking any such steps.

Taking a deep breath from my mouth, I followed closely by Ashta, trying my best to not use my nose. Not a soul could be seen nor heard. Merely slight splashes from whatever lived in the water, the depressed drips coming from nowhere, and the occasional hum you hear in silent places, otherwise stillness cried between the walls.

Then began the rhythmic echoing patters. Ashta quickly turned to me, her eyes shone with warning. My shaking hand tugged my hood down. The patters grew as we trotted on, the thuds of our horse's hoofs and the patters agonisingly waiting to meet. Getting closer, a long shadow began to appear on the wall, its master sinisterly hidden behind the bend.

A slight rattle and hiss scraped through the air as the lord of the moving shadow appeared. His head hanged to the side as if it were too heavy for its neck, with unnaturally large green eyes. My heart skipped a beat as he blinked, his eyelids sweeping from the sides rather than from top to bottom. Ashta did not stop, so neither did I. Staring as we brushed passed, his thin forked tongue thrashed slightly out of his mouth, and he began to follow after us.

I did not dare look back as the patters followed along. The image of his burning green eyes etched deeply into my own, slowly sliding its eyelids along the sides. A snake, perhaps a lizard. Patter patter it went. Hiss rattle. Patter patter.

Bong. The patters began to weaken as the sudden bongs ahead got louder. Bong, ominous whispers floated through the rotten air. Bong, a neigh, thuds of boots. Existences up ahead, and existence is what we got.

Beings stalking along like any other day. Horns, antlers, volcanic hair. A man came flying out of one of the doorways on the other side of the water, crashing down as a short and a giant man came out of the same doorway. "IF THERE'S A NEXT TIME YOUR DEAD!" Roared the short one with the voice of thunder.

"Don't you dare show your face here again!" Squeaked the large one.

I bit down on my lip, putting all my energy into not laughing as the high pitched squeak of the giant man's voice bounced off the walls. His arms the size of me seemingly becoming a mere joke as the little squeals of his vocal cords whined behind the short chubby man. As if sensing my distraction, Ashta lightly pinched my arm. *No distraction.*

We passed a doorway with a golden sign saying live, killed, or cooked ins. The smell of roasted meat escaped through the gaps of the door. My mouth drooled as Ashta tightly held on to my arm and dragged me and the horse I was riding. The savoury air retired behind us.

At last, we stopped at one of the doorways. A white door scratched up revealing dirty old wood beneath it. To its left a skeletal man sat like a limp rag doll, his eyes protruding from their sockets. Dark eye bags highlighted the bulging cheekbones that seemed to nearly cut through his frail skin.

Jumping off her horse, Ashta threw the reins to the sickly man and signaled to me to do the same. Then, she knocked on the door as I watched the lifeless man slowly blink, the only sign of him being alive.

Creeping open, an eye appeared behind the ajar door, a metal chain dangled in front, making sure it couldn't be forced open. "Yes?" Drawled the eye.

"We're here for Madam," whispered back Ashta.

"What Madam?" The eye questioned as it scraped its way down the top to the bottom of my skin.

"Madam Madam."

"She is not available," and with a swoop of the door, the eye disappeared.

Ashta banged on the door again with a huff. "Yes?" Returned the eye as the door slightly opened once more.

"We are here for Madam Madam!" She snapped.

"She is not available," the door closed swiftly, the dead looking man rasped a chuckle.

Once more ashta knocked on the door. "Yes?" The eye returned.

"We are here for Madam Madam," she whispered as she pulled something from inside her coat.

"Well, why didn't you say so!" Cried the voice happily.

Ashta rolled her eyes trying to hide the smile of triumph that flashed on her face. *Well, I guess they don't say money can buy anything for no reason.*

The door closed, the metal chain clanked, and a second later the door was thrown wide open. A short old lady stood in front of us, unusually square, almost cartoonish, with wide bug eyes. With a wrinkly brown robe thrown upon her curved body, she smiled showing off her strangely long teeth.

"Come in come in," she rasped as she snatched the money and wobbled back inside "close the door behind, lots of funny people out there."

We stepped inside, taking one last look outside at the strange man who seemed to have fallen asleep, I gently closed the door. The weirdly orange wooden floorboards creaked beneath our feet, a choir of damaged vocal cords. I bit the inside of my cheek as I tried to get used to its horrid sound.

The walls, dimly greenish grey, wore mould and rust as their overcoat. A mess of colours lay strewn on the sides of the hall, red, green, blue, with coins scattered over them. "Take a seat my little lovely dovelys, I just made cookies, fresh and warm and goooooooeyyyyyy," the lady hobbled along, throwing the coin behind her in the hallway then opening the kitchen door.

"It's ok, we're good," replied Ashta politely.

"Oh but you must! My special recipe," she smiled her blood red gums peeking through her widening smile.

"No no, really it's fine."

"Ah, children these days, so little manners, but who's to blame but ourselves? For we were the ones who made you this way," she sighed "now now do take a seat, how may I help you my little sparkly frogiesss!"

Sparkly froggies...?

"We have come to ask about a myth," Ashta said.

"It is not real."

"What is?" She asked.

"Myths aren't real" cackled the lady.

"Right... anyways have you heard of the land of humans?"

"Maybe, maybe not, we live in such a funny world do we not? Why, I must ask, why are so quiet?" She turned to me, her bug eyes wide open.

Tugging my hood, I looked at ashta who gave me a tiny nod, "uh, I don't have anything to say, madam." I murmured.

"Is that so? What a silly thing to say, you just said something!" She leaned over the table, her face inches away from mine "FLICK," she yelled suddenly as she threw my hood off.

"WHAT THE," I screeched my arms scrambling to get my hood up.

"That's more like it, use your vocal cords little sock pie, don't let them sweep you away. Though why should I care? You are a funny thing aren't you," she laughed.

"What on earth are you going on about?!" I snapped.

"Ehm," Ashta interrupted, "we are here on serious busine—"

"You are quite a rarity," the lady kept on going, "why look at your funny nose."

"What the heck is wrong with my nose?"

"What isn't wrong with your nose?"

"What...?"

A sudden shriek of laughter erupted from her mouth.

I looked at Ashta, my eyes filled with question marks. She grimaced and shrugged her shoulders in reply.

"Want a cookie?" The lady whispered.

"Uh, no thank you." I replied hesitantly, "can I ask you a question?"

"Oh go on my little bundle of fluffy pebbles, ask away."

"Right um thanks, so do you know about the world of humans?"

"Nope."

"Oh?" I looked back at Ashta in defeat as she rolled her eyes.

"Myths my darling, all hubble bubble." The women giggled.

"Well can you tell us about the myth?"

"Nope."

"Why not?" Asked Ashta.

"Because I don't know anything," she chuckled.

Ashta sighed as she rummaged through her pockets.

"Oh no need, I won't take your money."

"Why not?"

"Because I don't know, you should check your ears little lamb chops."

"Please, madam." Ashta sighed once more as she held her head.

"As you said it's merely a myth, one that I have no information on," she smiled placing a whole cookie in her mouth.

"But you know every damn thing!"

"Mhm thats — also a — myth," she mumbled pieces of the cookie flying out of her open mouth.

"Any bit of information, madam!" I implored.

"I gave you plenty of information wobbly munchkins, now come along I have work to do," she stood up, crumbs cascading down her robe onto the filthy floor.

"But you haven't answered anything!" Howled Ashta.

"Oh on the contrary little Miss rat whiskers, I've told you far too much. You really should go to the doctors and check your ears out."

"Madam please," I begged, "please Madam."

"Come on little darlings," she said as her strangely strong body pushed us through the way, "now now, it was lovely seeing you, do come again!"

Bang, the door closed shut as we stared outside in disbelief. The dead man snickered. "Well that was interesting," I whispered.

Ashta's hand rolled up into fists and looking up to me whispered back "I don't know what to do now Lana."

"What- I mean- it's ok, we'll find something else,"

She lowered her head, her hood shading her face from the world, "I'm sorry," she croaked.

"For what?"

She sighed.

"Ashta?" I repeated.

She took a deep breath, "nothing I'm just overwhelmed," and raising her head she smiled apologetically.

"Ashta."

"Mhm?"

"Thank you."

Whipping her nose, she chuckled "we haven't succeeded."

Suddenly, her words began to echo in my head. *haven't succeeded.* Gradually digging deeper into my brain, meandering into the hollows of my spine. *Failed.* The world engulfed around me as I realized. The tunnel we stood in seeming to get smaller and smaller, my vision began to project the dancing fear once more. His hollow eyes staring deeper and deeper, his mouth widening, becoming my whole vision.

Forever. Done. A thunder of despair rained down upon me, a volcanic eruption of centipedes slowly digging their way out of my guts. Done. Forever.

"We will—" I whispered in an almost trance like manner.

"Lana?" Someone called from afar.

I did not search for the caller, for who cares? It was all done. *Perhaps this is merely where I I'm meant to be, a place of creatures, my insanity being my special trait.* My hip seemed to fall apart into pieces, unable to hold both my body and mind, though the latter should have no weight, and yet it far outweighed the former.

Grief swapped places with the cells of my body, the death of my world, the death of my home, the death of the sky, the clouds, the moon. *The death of me, whatever I may be!*

A world of delusions. My world of delusions!

"Lana," the calls grew louder.

"Mhm?" I replied.

"There's still hope!" Ashta, the owner of the voice, encouraged.

Hope. Bitterness began to form in my mouth. *Such a disgusting term! A term used by those who do not see their delusions. A term filled with lies. Lies. Lies!*

Hope is but a fools curtain, see through without even the slight ability of obscuring light! A waste of damn time! How much is lost chasing the abyss?! Delusions! All merely delusions! A world of pure delusion!

My face drained as utter anguish, utter hopelessness, utter fear rampaged against the walls of my minds. What else was a delusion?! My being?! My self?! Delusions! Delusions!

"OY, SOBBY PANTS," a voice interrupted "take your damn horses I'm not a stable."

"Oh, he talks...." Muttered Ashta beneath her breath, "we're coming we're coming, come on Lana snap out of it."

****

The dreary ride home was merely that. Dreary.

The trees laughed at my failure, their bodies bent as they pointed at us with their branches. "The lost one," they cackled quietly as I drowned in a pit of dependance.

For that was all I could possible do now, depend, for who was I in this bizarre world? Or rather what was I?

A pathetic creature without a path. No where back, no where forward. A creature with the dire need to chain herself to the legs of another, for now that I had no path what else could I do but tether myself to the one person that understands? The one person by my side in the ocean of hundreds? Thousands? Perhaps millions?!

What am I in this world of absurdity?! Nothing if not for her! Oh how disgusting such feelings are, but I cannot lie her presence elevated me.

The thought of her leaving! *Ah what type of insoluble creature am I?!* O how truly lucky I was, to have someone in a such world!

"Thank you, Ashta." I whispered, a lump of gratitude forming in my throat.

"Hm?"

"Thanks," I reiterated

"For what?" She smiled.

"For being there."

"Of course Lana."

I whispered another thanks for how else could you communicate gratitude? Was there even a possible way to communicate such gratitude?

A breeze flowed between our hearts, transporting every minute feeling that couldn't possibly be communicated through words. A type of translation that

I could not even imagine existing. And yet accompanied by the sounds of our breathing, we trotted back home in the clouds of failure. The air seeming to spray a mist of anguish with each trot of the horse's hooves.

All was dull as we entered the castle, its giant hall seeming infinite after the grim sewers. Yet it did not sooth the despair that climbed to us.

Sliding off my cloak, something small glided down, barely emitting an audible scrunch as it gently touched the ground. Picking it and putting it up to my eye, I realized it was a delicately folded paper. Unwrapping it out of mere curiosity, my eyes fell upon a message written in scrawny handwriting "M.M 12AM come alone."

"Uh, Ashta?"

"I'm sorry Lana but I'm really tired, is it important?"

"No, but-"

"Then, tell me later," she said as she slumped off.

Perhaps it was a mistake and yet I had this strange urge to investigate the matter. *What's the worst that could happen?* The annoying part of my brain replied with *murder, torture, organ harvesting* but I prefer to ignore that part of my brain.

Obviously, the paper was from whoever wore this cloak beforehand but what if it wasn't? Was it for me? It belonging to Ashta seemed to be the most obvious conclusion, after all, it was her cloak.

Sighing, I pulled at the little message between my fingers. *M.M. Could it perhaps be Madam Madam? Had she snuck a message into my cloak? Why not just go and investigate?*

I made up my mind as I walked through the empty halls towards my room. *A nap would do me good as I wait for the moon to awaken.* Closing my eyes to the tune of the afternoon wind, I chuckled at my ludicrous idea.

Chapter 22

Awoken by a knock at my door, I was surprised to see the sun setting on the horizon, vibrant flames rolling through the soft blue sky. The hues of passion and anger, as if the sky could feel, feel ever so deeply, hoping for its weeping to be heard. Longing for its despair to be recognised.

"Yes?" I called out with my eyes fixated on the enchanting view.

The door opened and in walked the lady with green hair, Akhthar, wearing a slick suit. "Her royal highness invites you to dinner," she recited.

"Ok I'll be there," I replied, she stood emotionlessly for what seemed to be a century, waiting in pure silence, "uh do you need anything?" I asked.

"No."

"Then why are you waiting?"

"To take you to dinner," perhaps I imagined it, but it seemed like she could barely contain rolling her eyes.

"It's ok I know my way."

Tilting her head seemingly unsure for a second, she nodded and left. My eyes returned to the window containing the sky's burning tears. *Perhaps we see ourselves in the things around us.* I smiled as I got up, imagining myself as one of the sparks of the sky's burning heart.

Ethereal. I did not know the true meaning of the word till I walked down the hallway. Bestowed upon my eyes were the orange flames of the sunset flowing through the tall windows. An orchestra of light and dark as the walls between the windows contrasted the light with its lack of luminosity. Why did I think it was so pretty? The delicate swirls of glowing red, a wordless poem.

Entering the dining hall, I was met with a crashing wave of aromas. The spices filling the air, invited me in with such mannered courtesy, "you took your time," chuckled Ashta who sat waiting at the table, wearing a soft green dress.

"Have you not seen the sunset?" I grinned back.

"So easily distracted huh,"

"I melt at the sight of beauty," I laughed.

"Ah, so that's why it seems like you are so meek in my presence?" She smirked, "Sorry about earlier by the way, I could barely keep my eyes open," she began thoughtfully.

"Hm?"

"You wanted to tell me something earlier?"

Everything came rushing back like a slap to the face. 12AM. "Oh, um yeah but I don't remember what it was," I smiled, guilt building inside of me.

"Oh well," she shrugged, cutting into the steaming steak that had been placed on her plate, "do you have a hobby?"

"Hm?"

"A hobby?" She asked,

"Um, not really I guess." I replied.

Rolling her eyes she continued, "Well I realized I don't actually know a lot about you."

"I guess you're right," taking a break to chew, I titled my head in thought, "what's yours?"

"Oh..." She laughed, "I kinda like playing with animals."

"Animals?" I smiled.

"Mhm, barn animals."

"That's rather strange," I pushed another piece of meat into my mouth, delicious.

"Not really, I was sort of raised with barn animals."

"You? The princess?!" My eyes wrinkled into a confusion.

"Yeah," She laughed, "it's sort of a sporting thing."

"Like dog training?"

"Sure, you could say that," she smiled.

"What do you like about it?" I asked, absentmindedly returning to the masterpiece that sat on my plate.

"Well, there's a sort of serenity in it, almost as if you are in control."

"The training part?" I smiled, shaking my head.

"No, or actually yes" Chuckled Ashta, "perhaps control isn't the best word, but there's this sort of freedom you know?"

"In having control?"

"Yeah,"

"Sounds like you have a problem," I joked.

"You know what I mean." She shook her head laughing.

"Not really, but it sounds nice." I smiled as a silence fell like a soft blanket on a winter's day. Cozy and calm, not a slight bit awkward. The aroma that had greeted me now pirouetted on my tongue to the tune of our steady breaths. "Is this ins?" I asked.

"I believe it's beef," Ashta replied, her eyes marveling at her own plate.

I noticed that beef was a lot more chewier and lacked the subtle taste unique to ins.

My mind wandered to my night plans. A trickle of guilt and doubt ran through my spine. Why did I feel so bad? Ashta will understand. You'd think the way I was overthinking that I had murder on my mind or something. I scoffed at myself and the brain I had that seemed to constantly be on overdrive.

"Lana," Spoke Ashta.

"Mhm," I mumbled, my mouth stuffed.

"What will you do if you can't return?'

"What?" I blurted.

"Sorry, it's a silly question,"

"No no, I just, I don't know," I replied, my chest heavy as if someone had knocked the air out of my lungs.

"You can stay with me,"

Stay with her? like a dying thing in need of a saviour, perhaps that was what I truly was. Nothing more than a dying thing... in need of a saviour. Ah how pitiful I sound. How truly pitiful! but one cannot blame me, for hope is but a delusion, and not even the deepest of delusions could possibly make sense of anything in this world. In me.

Was there even anything back home for me?

I scraped the remains of my plate, perhaps I'm merely insane. A lost insanity. One tainted with disorientation, pure concentrated disorientation.

"I'm going to do more thinking about this situation," declared Ashta as she pushed her seat out, "have a goodnight."

"You too." I replied lost in my own world.

Getting out of my own seat, I watched as Ashta's white locks disappeared behind the door.

Chapter 23

I could not help but laugh at my own anxiety as I sat watching the clock ticking away. The moon had risen, beautifully shimmering against the never ending satin sky. With the sounds of the soft clouds whistling, I sighed feeling stuck in a never ending second.

Tick tock. Tick tock. *What does one do as one waits?* Tick tock. Tick tock. I laid my head on the cool glass window, my cheek tingling at the contrasting temperature. Tick tock. Tick tock. I sighed staring at the moon who had seen it all. The moon who had been looked upon by the people of the past and of the future.

As my mind pondered through an abyss of curiosity, the clock struck 10. 2 hours left. My legs, that were itching to move two seconds before, became two sacks of jiggly potatoes as the nerves began to set in. I got up and jiggled my legs.

Out the door and through the hall, I slowly dragged my feet till I stood once again in front of the giant exit. I fastened the blue cloak that I had just grabbed from the hangar and stood hesitantly. Grabbing the handle, I froze remembering Ashta knocking in a pattern.

1 2.. 1 2.. 1 2.. 1 2 3 4. The door opened. Purple cloaks. Wolf eyes. Standing high, I walked out, their eyes following as if I were scratching my nails against a chalkboard. Parasites seemed to gnaw at my stomach, having a feast upon my anxiety. Time couldn't possibly go slower.

They did not move, unlike my racing heart. With triumph coursing through my anxiety ridden body, I urged myself to go on till I was out of sight.

For some reason, I had thought there'd be some sort of ride at the same place we were presented horses. Contemplating whether I should go on or search for a horse, a thought popped into my mind, *perhaps I could go back and ask the wolf eyed men.* Of course, that thought left as fast as it had entered.

Looking back at the castle, which seemed to drown

in black rather than grey as it did in the morning, I wondered if I could walk through a forest in pitch dark. *Do I have the time to go search for the stables? Probably not.*

My shoes eerily clicked on the stone pathway slicing the silence of the night, as if it were a warrior shrouded by the clouds which still whistled their sad tune. The lavender's aroma, once again, swam through the cold air, though it did not seem so calming as the darkness shadowed their delicate colours. The grass that once whispered their rumours lay asleep quietly, or perhaps, their fear had finally come true, perhaps now they were nothing more than empty vessels, unable to see, unable to think. Nothing but grass.

From afar an owl began to whisper, snatching silence's sword, as if to call upon any saviour that may be standing on the land. The trees, seeming much larger in size, amplified even the slightest allophone heard from the owl's hum, perhaps the leaves rustled with ever intonation, but who's to say? For no eyes that could see were present amongst those trees.

I must admit, I have very little sense of direction, however, the way through the forest was pretty straightforward, even for someone who was born with the opposite of a compass embedded into the depths of their skin. Not literally of course, though sometimes I do wonder.

As the trees began to give way, a new world opened up. An uncountable world of infinite beauty, a world that could not be walked upon, a world utterly devoid of atrocities. The world of stars. Shimmering, almost unrealistically, against the dark. One cannot help but wonder how they do not become utterly engulfed by the darkness as one watches them embellish the sky.

Using all their luminosity to show the pitch black sky, it seemed that they had no more strength to light up anything more and, very much to my dismay, not a singular lamp gave way at the edge of the village.

My feet moved along only by sensing the sodden bridge beneath them. Though the lake obviously still was there, it made no sound to prove its existence, nor did the rest of the village for that matter. Only the presence of utter silence could be heard followed by the few taps from my feet every now and then, though they were nearly impossible to hear as the soaked bridge dulled their sounds.

I continued, the image of the place during the day leading me, even spurring me on, picturing the mystical mountains, now blanketed, the stars unable to stop them from being flooded by the dark.

The village seemed to have far more twists and turns than I had remembered, probably because I was mindlessly following Ashta on a horse last time. The time began to pass as I aimlessly roamed the sleeping streets. The bottom of my cloak dragged on behind me, damp from the wet bridge, mopping the dark floor. A little scratching sound started to follow, my mind raced back to the creepy lizard man but was immediately calmed as it realized it was merely a random twig that had decided to join my soggy outfit.

I came to a stop. A myriad of clocks stared at me as I stood outside their little shop, 11:30 PM they all ticked, beating together tucked in their haven.

At that point i had concluded that a wrong turn must have trespassed through my way for I did not remember seeing a shop of clocks before.

Frustrated, I deeply inhaled, how on earth did I think I'd find my way? I sat on the cold rugged floor, resting my head on the window of the clock shop. The clocks, vibrating the glass, seemed to want to give me a concussion. *Reason of death? Shaken by clocks.* Smiling at my stupidity, a faint sweet smell wafted through the air. The dying remnants of caramel nuts.

Guided by my nose like an oversized dog, I began to follow the smell of which now smelled more like Willy Wonka's vomit. Not that I've ever smelt anything of the sort, but I imagine having a diet of pure sugar would give a similar result.

The floor murmured beneath my feet as I scuttled along. My eyes squinting in hopes of being able to guide the soft light of the stars. Slithering through the air, the smell strengthened with every step, till at last, I found myself standing in front of the small wooden cart. Empty. Entirely devoid of life. A sad stall bathing in its rotting odour, sulking over its once bewitching scent. "Don't worry cart your time shall shine once more in the morning," I whispered to it as if it would understand.

"What type of person talks to a stall?" came a mocking rumble from behind, forcing a yelp out of my throat.

Instinctively, I swirled to face the sound with my hand on my rushing heart. My widened eyes hid beneath the hood of my cloak. Sitting lazily on the opposing wall was a tall man hidden beneath his own cloak. With one leg laid straight on the wall and the other dangling on the side, his back slouched onto the taller wall next to it.

I began to walk away in silence but was interrupted by the same voice, "where are you going?"

My gut pushed my legs forward in urgency. *Do not reply, do not reply, do not reply*, echoed through my head as my heart pounded. Suddenly, a shocking jolt ran through my arm. An icy thunder barely lasting a second yet forcing another yelp to escape from me as if I had been zapped with an electric wire. A freezing electric wire.

"WHAT THE HELL," I instinctively thundered turning back around, my fear turning into a second of anger.

His head rolled back with pure laughter burying all traces of bravery I had spawned. His unnaturally white teeth glimmered, catching the moonlight as it lit the bottom half of his face that was not covered by his cloak. "So you speak," he chuckled, "though that wasn't very polite of you," he yawned as if getting bored.

I stood silently trying to figure out what just happened, *did he have some bizarre taser?* I decided it was a bizarre taser, "well it wasn't very nice of you to tase me" I snapped back.

"Tase you?" and once more he fell into a fit of laughter.

Turning around, I began to walk away once more, "wait a second," I heard, followed by the sound of a swift landing.

I ran, adrenaline taking over. Nausea began to fill my throat as my heart pumped with fear. My foot crashed one in front of the other and yet, only a few meters away, my knees buckled beneath me as another sharp icy jolt ran through me. The palms of my hands propelled onto the rough street in an attempt to break my fall.

"I said wait," peered the tall man above me. My eyes welled up from the stinging pain in my hands, "who are you?" He asked nonchalantly.

"None of your damn business," I replied with my teeth clenched.

He plopped down in front of me, peering at the visible part of my face. Suddenly, he flicked my hood off. "HEY," I shouted as I tried to get up, fighting against my burning scraped knees.

Grabbing my wrist in a deathly grip, he dragged me back down, "STOP IT," I screamed.

"Be quiet people are asleep," he replied calmly.

"LEAVE ME THE HELL ALONE," I screamed, trying to get up once more.

"Shush," he yanked me down again, this time alongside jolt of horrid coldness, turning my vein into pure ice a second. "Stop," I cried, lumped on the floor in front him.

He sat silently with his legs crossed as if lost in thought, "who are you?" He began once more.

Sitting silently on the cold street, all was silent but my snuffled tears. "Who are you?" He asked again, his voice calm, riddled with authority.

"Lana," I whispered in a choke.

Grabbing my face like an artifact, he lifted it towards the moonlight. His fingers were icicles upon my bare skin, embedding it's cold as if they were crawling parasites slithering within. "Lana?" He said, twisting my head left and right.

"Yes, please let me go," I squeaked, fear taking over my pride.

His eyes transfixed on my face, he gripped my lower arm with his free hand and pulled it to his nose, "what— what— please stop," I wept.

Squirming as his freezing fingers dug into my skin, every cell in my body trembled with terror, as he smelt my wrist. Lowering his eyes, he inhaled once more, as if I were a drug. "What are you?" he finally said seriously, letting go of my face while his other still gripped my arm.

"I- I-," my mind raced through a flurry of nothingness, jumbled thoughts swam through an abyss of panic.

"What are you?" He repeated with irritation.

"I don't know," I cried "I don't know, please I didn't do anything, let me go," Blubbering, tears ran down my exposed face.

"How did you get here?"

"I- I don't know- I'm meeting someone- and the castle-," I incoherently jabbered, a cascading jumble of words falling out of my mouth.

"The castle?" He leans in, "Who owns you?"

"What," I stammered.

"Who owns you?" He crinkled his nose.

"I- no one."

"Don't lie to me," his voice slithered through the air like a snake.

"I'm not, I'm not."

"Who owns you," he growled.

"Ow, please, you're hurting me," my wrists throbbed, the blood blocked by his fingers.

Standing up, he held my arm tighter and dragged me off the floor. "Please don't, please, honestly I-I-" I whimpered, "please I have to meet someone."

"And who on earth would meet you," he sneered.

"Wh- what?" I croaked, "look I'm with princess Ashta, please let me go."

He stopped and looked down at me. Pure laughter came rumbling out of his mouth slicing the plaguing silence, his chest heaved beneath his cloak, and he began to drag me forward once more. "Look, look," I begged, "I have a royal medallion."

The piece of metal hung around my neck shone in my free hand as I lifted it up. The hairs on my neck rose and a shiver ran through my back as a smirk grew on his face. The air seemed to grow colder as he lifted his hood to get a better look at the medallion.

His eyes... A bolt of ice ran through my body, stronger than before. Searing pain. I gasped for air.

I stared into his eyes as the world began to darken. Ice burrowing between my once warm flesh. His eyes were all I could see until everything became nothing. My chaotic thoughts silenced. My fear murdered. His eyes becoming a dream. His eyes. His purple eyes. Purple eyes...

Chapter 24

Something crashed against my body, pain shot through muscles I never knew existed. The floor rumbled beneath my back. *What happened? Where was I?*

I got up onto my hands and knees as they fought against the vibrations slamming through my bones. While trying to balance, my eyes blinked wildly trying to be useful in the dark. A thin shard of light sparkled through a gap above me though it was too pale to enlighten my eyes as to where I was. I brushed my hands on the ceiling above my head, wincing as a splinter embedded itself into my already sore finger. Wood. *A coffin?*

The world began to swirl as panic began to set in. *Of course, of course, I was dead this whole time.* Nausea grated my veins, peeling them into shreds of tissue soaked in the bloody bath of all my fears. The irony of it all, *attending my own funeral!* Tears sprouted from my eyes. I was Dead. Gone!

Though death seems such a grave answer to one's insanity, I began to smile. *Dead! Gone! So this is death! You're still awake when you're dead! How the living world would rejoice to hear of such details!*

Perhaps it was all nothing more than a hallucination, ah but alas by the time I had reached that conclusion my brain had woken up and reached the realisation that I was in fact awake *because* I was alive.

I suddenly fell back as the movement stopped. Scrambling back to my knees, murmured whispers began through the air. I strained my ears in hopes of hearing what was being said but alas, it was as if I was listening to a broken radio.

Then the movement began again, launching me onto my face. I got myself up once more and tried pushing the walls. The hardwood stood solemnly beneath my palm, unwilling to budge. Moving my hand to the roof, I lightly pushed it up and was met with a cascading waterfall of moonlight pouring through the crack I had opened.

Peering out, a blurred painting of green lay in my sight. Wind blew against my naked eyes as I swerved them to the left to find the back of a running horse and a leg dancing to its rhythm. To the right was nothing but darkness between the blurred painting of the forest. Trying to deduce where I was, I focused attempting to un-blur the trees but the cold air whipped at my eyes. Icy tears ran down my bloodshot eyes as they were forced to close.

I sat back down, surely this wouldn't lead to anything good. My mind went to Ashta, *how would I explain this? Who said she'll find out?* The likelihood of me returning seemed low, but I wasn't dead, and had they wanted me dead they would have done so by now. Trafficking? Kidnapping? Ransom?

My mind flashed back to the tall man who laughed at the mention of Ashta's name. *The damn bastard.* Yet this revelation slightly relieved me, there was a chance I would return safely.

Accordingly, my heart choked at the thought of Ashta floored with fear, disgust flew into my lungs alongside the suffocating air. Clenching my teeth, I lifted the roof once more and pushed it open. Its rusty bolts heaved silently. Not having the ability to fall smoothly on its own, the lid stood upright.

Looking behind, I gathered the rider was not the tall man by his different build. I moved swiftly. He did not notice my slight rattles as the wind hid me in its choir.

The harsh wind blew against me, transforming my hair into dancing tentacles swinging behind me. My nose burnt as it breathed in the cold night air while being stabbed by the sharp wind. I took a deep breath, closed my eyes, then jumped.

Time is a funny thing, passing as you blink, while other times, fumbling through space with the speed of the moon phases. Experiencing the latter, my arm finally bashed onto the ground. My body pummeled along the wet grass as the carriage became smaller in the distance.

Finally coming into contact with the dirt, my hands began to sting once more as I lifted myself off the ground. The sound of dull crickets filled the air, gaining bravery from the dying sound of the horse hooves upfront. The air, chilly against my face, made me want to curl up into a ball of blankets.

Beginning to walk the way the carriage went, the twisting trees began to let go of each other's arms, leaving the group embrace. My eyes strained to see what was beyond the thinning trees but to no avail.

What time was it? Probably way too late to go to the stupid meeting point, not that I knew the way, my only directions being the trodden path.

Bellow the starry night, my feet dragged as they begged to be propped onto fluffy pillows. The air continued to whistle with its choir of nature. Tears began to slip down my face though my feet did not stop. I cried silently. My brain anguished and my legs aching. No way to go but forwards behind the long gone carriage.

Emptiness. Numbness. The blurring trees attempting to distract. *Why continue?* I let the air engulf me, embrace me, conceal me. I imagined it injecting warmth into me.

It filled me with nothing. Nothing, but air.

I continued, my feet beginning to lose feeling. My body shivered with the memory of the icy shock. I continued. *Why?*

My eyes began to slow, losing sight. My ears began to distort, loosing sound. All became one with my feet, one step after the other. The ground seemed to fade into the trees as the trees began to fade into time. Minutes? Hours? Time did not exist.

****

The castle. My eyes focused. I found myself in front of the castle, or rather, the back of the castle. Nevertheless, a numb type of relief blossomed through my aching body like the first spring flower. *Home. When did I begin considering this place home?*

Though I was obviously on the castle premises, the castle still seemed far being blocked by various grey buildings similar to the castle itself. I ventured ahead. A low neigh rumbled somewhere close by. The stables. I made a mental note.

My senses, surprisingly aware, listened to the air around me. Traveling through the air were the questionings of the night owls. Pondering the mysteries of this reality. Who? Who whoo? *Who indeed wise old owl, who indeed.* Though I could not answer, my ears held onto their questions as if they were my saviours, their curiosity a comforting blanket to hide behind, though no blanket has the ability to stop a knife.

A light whisper followed, unfortunately not an answer to the owl's questions, and though I was on castle grounds I could not help but run in a silent flurry. Ducking into one of the barns, I stood behind the door clenching my heart.

All was pitch dark. An intermediate drip echoed through the silent darkness. Plink plink plip, it sang hitting what sounded like a puddle.

Placing my hand on the wall in search of a light switch, I took a step. The floor brimmed with warm water, slowly soaking through my shoes. I took a deep breath and kept walking, my hand tracing along the rigid wall. Water continued to ooze into my shoes, its warmth pleasing my freezing toes.

Fumbling, my feet flew behind me as I slipped. My hands, flailing wildly for something to hold on to, pummeled into a splash beneath me. I held my breath. Begging from the very depths of my heart that my fall wasn't loud enough to be heard outside.

I waited. My heart quivered.

After a minute of nothing but the sound of my volcanic heart against the agitating drips of water, I got up, wiping my face with my hands, noticing it's wetness only after it contacted my face.

I stood silently. Plink. Plink.

Slowly turning around, raising my hands in front of me in attempt to feel something other than the wall I left behind my back, I began to shuffle forward. The water slightly rose with each step though barely noticeable if not for the added warmth it gave me. I silently scooped the warm water with the tip of my feet, allowing it to travel backwards up to my ankles. The warmth felt heavenly.

Bump. My hands landed upon a warm pillar, the warmth seeping into my fingers. Hesitating, I positioned my body onto the pillar and hugged it. The heat that first entered my fingers slid down my body. I shivered as it began to caress my frozen bones. A singular teardrop fell from my check onto the soaking floor below. *Warmth. Heat.*

A calming sensation wrapped around my body, goosebumps ran down my arms blanketed by the pleasant temperature. *Why must the cold be so agonising?* I wanted nothing more than to stay unmoving forever allowing the radiator to continue echoing through my heart.

Click. A halo of white light flickered illuminating my eyes red for a second, then darkness.

Click. More red, then darkness. I blinked in bewilderedness. An urgency to run came down on me as the warmth of the radiator begged me to stay.

Click. Prepared this time, I swerved my head in hopes of catching sight of something. More red. Darkness.

Click. This time the light did not close. Echos of laughter rumbled between all four corners of the barn. My eyes widened in horror. The world around danced in disfiguration. Red. Red. Red.

My hands. Red. Thickly coated with red. Glistening red like liquid dripped from my fingers like blood. Blood? Shaking, I brought my hands to my eyes, my ears beginning to pound like the cries of soldiers going into war.

My eyes began to unfocus from my hands, redirecting my vision to what stood in front of me. "I - I – I..." whispered jitters escaped my mouth as I fell back at the sight of what was keeping me warm.

"It's a beauty isn't it." Someone cackled, their voice sounding like it came from another planet.

A large slab of meat hung upside down, feet hanging from metal shackles. Skinless, headless, arms hanging stiffly. My head began to swirl as I shuffled backwards in panic, splashing in the water, no the blood. *Blood. Blood. Blood.* A pungent metallic smell began to choke me. *Blood. Blood everywhere.* I began to wipe my hands on my chest in a panic, pulling at my clothes in rapid confusion, a cry escaped my mouth. Tears, screams. *Blood. Blood. Blood.*

I couldn't breathe, as if an elephant sat on my lungs. *Blood.* It was all blood. *Must get this blood off.* A movement caught my eyes. A ball came rolling in front of me. *What was that?*

A head.

I sat frozen as the sound of laughter echoed once more. The head staring at me with empty eyes. I couldn't move, frozen. "What.. what is that," I whispered hoping my thoughts were wrong.

The body dangled in front of me, a mixture of pink and red flesh still swinging from my embrace. The head sitting in front, skin still attached. Rigor mortis, not a radiator.

"What do you think?" Someone replied sinisterly.

"No," I winced, hunching my shoulders, "No no no," throat croaking, eyes beginning to puff as a floodgate of tears ran down my face.

"Say it," an almost animalistic voice scratched the air.

"NO!" I lashed, scrambling onto my feet.

The warm bloodied floor sent my leg flying beneath me, a waterfall of blood rained down on my tangled body laying hopelessly in the red pool. "No," I sobbed, as I lay beneath the body, its arms dangling inches from my face.

The head stared into my blood soaked face, no sympathy, no emotion, nothing left inside there.

"No need to make a fuss," the voice laughed, "it's only a human."

The world blackened in front of my eyes, my fears echoing around me. The words "It's only human" seemed to bounce from wall to wall, scrambling into my ears, agonisingly mincing my brain into shreds.

"Human. Human. Human." Echoed the room.

"Human?" I whispered in disbelief.

"Human. Human. Human. Hum-ins—"

"Hum… Ins?"

"Ins. Ins. Ins." the walls screeched with laughter.

"Fascinating creature," the voice whispered "almost in-human." Giggling.

I slowly turned around. My heart sank as the man peered into my face, hunger swimming in those purple eyes. The man with the purple eyes. Or were they red? "Red, red, red," echoed the walls.

"Apparently, you *are* my little sister's *friend*," he smirked, his eyes filled with amusement.

Getting up, the hanging flesh grazed my back, the smell seeming to grow by the second. Blood splashed around me in slow motion as the world swirled.

"One step" whispered the walls, "come on."

Gravity seemed to have increased its pull as my feet swayed beneath me, the oxygen in the air feeling too large to fit into my nostrils. The blood soaked floor appeared to merge with the whispering walls, or was it the blood whispering? "Don't step on us!" They screamed as they slipped me off my feet.

My face plummeted to the ground sending a vibration of pain through my nose. A metallic taste began to swim on my tongue, my own blood, or perhaps from the person whose blood dripped like an hourglass still swinging from the ceiling. "Are you hungry?" Someone said as the world seemed to disappear in front of my eyes.

Chapter 25

Suddenly awake, my body heaved, convulsing what seemed to be the very organs out of my body. Vomit spewed across the ground as I tried to catch my breath, burning tears ran down my face, begging for air.

The world was silent as I stared at my concoction bubbling on the ground. I was in a small stone room on a bed of straw, no light but the weak glimmers that found their way through the head shaped window. Isolated.

There is something so profound in being isolated. A sense of dread you can say. It is, of course, not isolation itself that carries the dread but the distractions it takes away, giving the brain freedom to run wild, allowing the deepest darkest ideas to bubble to the surface. What once was forgotten, stimulated from the death of movement. Though, was there any difference from what was?

Sitting in the dark, I wondered, *if I take a few steps, could I submerge into its pure nothingness?* Become one with the atoms that intertwine the heavy air. *Was I not always isolated? Is this physical cage really the beginning of my confinement?* Of course not, I have always been isolated. My brain, the prison of my body, and my body, the prison of my brain. Something curious stuck in a meat sack you could say.

Isolated in a third cage. The cage of the mind. The cage of the body. The cage of this location.

I made my way to the little window hoping to gouge my whereabouts. Standing on tiptoes, I gazed out.

I slammed my eyes shut. The contents of my body began to rise as if pushing to bleed out through the holes of my eyes. I reopened them, wide now in fear or, perhaps, regret at ruining the little peace the vomit filled room contained.

Staring back at me were beings, hundreds, no thousands, in tattered robes. Beings. Human looking beings, squatting next to each other in fenced pens made of moldy wood. *Animal pens.* Climbable if not jumpable, pushable even because of the mould having eaten up the wood, a slight push would have turned it into mush.

I rubbed my eyes. Exhaustion.

How much I yearned for all to be nothing and nothing to be all, though I cannot comprehend the existence of nothing, every organ in my body wished it could indulge in its perplexity.

Or perhaps to be a rock, no, a pebble, living beside a creek, splashes sizzling on me as I bake beneath the sun. Unaware of my home. Unaware of my surroundings. Unaware of the world. Unaware of my own damn existence!

The people stared back, wide eyed, "hello?" I whispered, "excuse me?"

They huddled closer together. Silent but the shuffles of their rags against the stone floor. Their faces drained, smudged with dirt, devoid of life. They were humans.

DING, the sound of clanking metal rang through the hall, or a more accurate name, the barn.

In seconds the people seemed to forget of my existence as they ran to the side, pushing and shoving for a space closer to what seemed to be a long cylinder. A trough. From pipes above, poured a thick yellow green liquid. Hands flew maniacally, grappling at chunks, their eyes wild with hunger though their body seemed to signify otherwise. A child drowned his face into the mixture, the lady next to him using both her hands to scoop the mush up to her face as if it was her last meal. Another dragged both her full hands to move her disheveled hair off her face, strands becoming soaked with the concoction, embellishing her hair with a crown of chunks.

Nausea began to knead its way from the pit of my stomach, rising to fill my head as I watched the thousands climb on top of each other to reach, what seemed to be, an endless trough. Gurgling, inhuman noises escaped their mouths as they gasped for air.

Splat. I looked away from the window. There stood my own mini trough, fresh with the chunky yellow green liquid. My stomach flipped, performing a gymnastics routine as the fumes intermingled with my vomit. A smell I cannot quite describe. Perhaps pickled sardines, rotten eggs, expired Camembert, the bitterness of a game cartridge aka, denatonium benzoate, and hints of something sickeningly sweet.

I turned back to the window, ignoring the small swimming pool of atrocities. Their trough seemed to have re-filled. A shiver ran up my spine.

Strangely hollow eyes sunken into obese faces, these people looked normal, or as normal as one can get in this place.

I had a premonition of what I was looking at but deeply buried such thoughts. One cannot be blamed. To see your own people in such a state.

"Perhaps they're prisoners," I whispered to myself, *criminals?*

I thought that perhaps it was the human section, it would only be fair to isolate them from the others considering the lack of advantages, putting us at risk.

My eyes darted at the short wooden fences "Excuse me," I whispered once more, receiving no reply.

I lay my hand on the door and shook though to no avail. I went to the other side of the room and ran towards the door, crushing my shoulder. A sharp pain ran down my arm as I looked at my failed attempt. *Damn it. If only they had put me in a fence like them.*

The smell seemed to get worse alongside the acceleration of my heart. Reality began to set in. The walls seemed to close in on me, slowly scraping the floor, screeching itself into a claustrophobic tightness around my chest. I wanted to leave.

My arms shook as I tried once more to shake open the door. Pulling the bolts and poking the screws, my fingernails fit perfectly into the jagged part of the latter. I began to turn my hand like a screwdriver. Not budging, I pushed further. A slight ripping sound echoed alongside my whimper as the bolt teared my fingernail. Beginning to bleed as it exhibited my raw flesh, I stared at it clenching my teeth, almost grinding them back into my gums. I slightly pulled the nail backwards against itself. Thin layers of meat stretched from the sides, burning and pulsating with my frantic heart.

A creaking sound vibrated from afar, though close enough for it to potentially be in the barn. I looked back out of the window, my finger still throbbing. The humans had stopped eating. The people, I mean, stopped eating. Pushing one another in frantic hysteria. Splatters of food flew onto the floor as they fought to hide behind one another. Children were wide eyed with fear and yet soundless as they were crushed behind adults.

Footsteps began to ring, getting louder with each step. The people huddled. Fear converged with the air. I began to feel prickles of uncertainty.

Three men came into the view of my window, I lowered my head, leaving only my eyes peeking through, though they were probably aware of me being there.

All wearing white jackets, they strolled eyeing the heard in the pens. The first, with a double chin and badly shaven mustache, opened the gate to the pen on the far right of what can be seen from my window, leaving me without the ability to see them as they scuttled off to the far left corner. A piercing screech jumped off the walls following a crash and a skin crawling chuckle. "Quick," the second man snapped agitated.

"Live a little," the first rolled his eyes as he came out of the pen dragging the human who crowned herself with the chunks of food, now a dribble of blood accompanying it on her forehead.

The frizz on her head twitched as she whimpered. "Shut up!" The man growled, dragging her harder.

"We are on a tight schedule, do not play around!" Hissed the second.

"Come hold it," ordered the first to the third as he rolled his eyes.

Walking over, the third grabbed it, I mean her, by the arms and dragged her onto the floor, leaving her sprawled on her stomach spastically squirming, her spine inhumanly jumping up and down. He then sat on the back of her knees, her arms still held back, and nodded to the first guy, "ready."

Animalistic screams flew out of her mouth as well as my own as the first man grabbed her by the nape of her neck. His fingers digging into her skin, he lifted her head upwards, pulled out a curved knife and slashed the left side of her neck.

Blood gushed, spurted onto his perfectly white jacket, a peaceful smile drawn onto his splattered face as he watched the lady jerking, gasping as she attempted to inhale like she was drowning in an invisible ocean. Inhuman gargles swarmed out of her mouth, her eyes rolled in disarray, her wheezes begging for her windpipe to reconstruct itself.

30 seconds. 30 seconds of torture, then sleep embraced her into the arms of her own blood.

The other humans huddled as if they had merely gotten a little jump scare. The floor underneath me, however, seemed to swallow me whole as I stood, mouth agape. I clutched my own throat and stepped backwards in slow motion, the very soul of my body seemingly leaving this world.

They sang as they tied her feet and swung her up a piece of metal.

Her body hung like a sleeping bat.

The limp body swung, blood draining out like a luscious waterfall. *Red, beautifully red.* The door opened, I think. *Red, red, and the fresh smell of copper!* "How beautiful such things are!" I might have ludicrously laughed.

"What is it doing?" I think someone said, a very far voice.

Her face lay beautiful, even upside down, a beauty she did not possess before. Thick with the kisses of bloodied pain, dripping like honey made with blood soaked roses.

"Leave," another voice echoed.

"To sleep?" I replied to the low voice.

I wait for it,
Its soft hand caressing mine,
As it pulls me through a wispy abyss,
felt but never seen nor heard.

Closing my eyes knowing all is gone,
That death himself has come to claim my
weakened soul,
To set me free into the nothingness that I cannot
begin to comprehend nor ever behold.

Show me,
Show me nothing,
Show me a stretching abyss of air,
a vacuum filled with nothing but silence,
No colour,
no smell,
Show me nowhere.

But that is not nothing, is it?
the stretching abyss,
the silence,
the lack of colour,
the lack of smell,
There is always something waiting amidst.

So I beg the buttery hand to show me the way,

"Not now," it whispers.
"When?"
"Sometime, somewhere."
"But what is it," I ask.
"Nothing your mind will ever understand," it
replies.
"Please"
And with a sigh, it says "look through your arm
perhaps that will calm your mind."
"But I have no eyes on my arms."
"And what do you see?"

Nothing,
Still, the abyss exists,
barely breathing,
yet it inhales,
something exists I simply can not comprehend.

What is nothing?
How can it be?
When nothing is something.

"Lana?"

How weak must the mind be?

Chapter 26

"You know, this is rather funny." Said the man sitting in front of me, the purple eyed man with locks of snow, "you're absolutely mad."

I did not respond.

"But I don't blame you, what Ashta did was very wicked."

My eyes lit up to the sound of a friend though I still stayed silent, exhaustion having taken full possession of me.

"I have a feeling your quite lost, or perhaps you've pieced some stuff together. See, I'm on the edge really, I cannot lie, I ardently enjoy having fun and yet both options seem so amusing!" He reclined laughing as if having said a joke. "I could leave you utterly in the dark orrrrr, drum roll please, I could show you! Isn't it such a marvelous idea?"

He paused expecting an answer, my mind only responding by seeing thick drops of red sliding down his stark white hair.

"Argh you are so dull, I'm going to go with the second option! Oooooh but first are you hungry?"

I was. Starving even.

Ignoring my silence, he calls for dinner to be served. Steaming rice, fried vegetables, and the swirling smell of sizzling meat swam through the air. "Eat! Eat!" He urges as he starts guzzling his own.

I was not tied up. My legs were free to do as they pleased, but the very nerves in my body could not move, no, they *would* not move. Tired, I was so so tired.

I picked up my spoon, sliding a bit of everything into it, and placing it in my mouth.

"Chew! Chew! Chew!" echoed the walls.

But I'm so tired.

A single tear drop rolled down my eye.

"Oh don't cry darling! Here, let's watch the movie right now." The purple eyed man said gently as he picked up a remote, "eat before it gets cold!"

My body, a slush of ice, burned inside out as the meat and rice sat in my mouth, only having the strength to chew every 20 seconds.

A screen popped out from somewhere in the room. A pregnant women and a man smiled, both with stark white hair, their eyes purple, filled with hopes and dreams. The next clip rolls, the women and man again, this time holding a baby, purple eyes and white hair.

Clip 3, the women is pregnant again, the man stood besides her, smile wide, with a 2 year old boy in his arms.

Clip 4, the now 3 year old with the newborn in his lap.

Clip 5, the now 6 year old dancing with the now wobbling three year old.

Clip 6, the family eating dinner.

Clip 7, the mother and father filling forms.

Clip 8, the now 8 year old getting a vaccine shot as his now 5 year old sister watched, tears brimming in her eyes.

Clip 9, a school play.

Clip 10, horse riding.

Clip 11, a party.

Clip 12, a tantrum.

Clip 13, dentist appointment.

My plate was nearly empty. Pieces of meat wriggled in between my teeth, the aftertaste fuelling my nausea.

Clip 14, the mother happily asks behind the camera, "what are you doing guys?"

"Ashy is gonna make dinner all by herself!"

"And who's going to teacher her?"

"Me!" Cheered the boy, as the dad fluffed his hair besides him.

"How old are you Ashta?" The mother points the camera at the girl.

"8!"

"Wowwww," the mother and father sang their praises.

"And what are you going to make?" Asked the dad.

"Your favourite right?" Chipped in the mum.

Beaming the child squealed, "Ins! I'm gonna make Ins!"

Clip 15: 8 year old Ashta sits on the neck of a child, no older than her, her squeals of joy drowning his cries of fear as she badgers a blunt knife in and out of his neck. In and out. In and out. In and out as he gurgles blood, fighting to stay alive, flopping around like a fish out of water.

"Haha look mummy!"

"Well done darling!"

My head lolled sideways, my neck losing strength to stay upright.

Clip 16: the same child dangled upside down from the ceiling, the blood already drained out of his body, little Ashta scraping her knife against his skin.

"don't cut off the meat," her dad chirps as he holds his own knife, "let me help."

"No!" She squealed as she continued to messily skin the child.

Why do things never end?

Clip 17: the family now sat at the dining table.

"What are we waiting for?"

"My ins! My ins!" Ashta squeals.

"I taught her," the boy barges his way into view with a beaming face.

"Where's your ins Ashta?" The dad asks with pride.

"With the chef! With the chef!" She cheered, as a group of servers walked in, head held high.

My lungs seemed to have shrunken as it wheezed for air.

Clip 18: the family feasted.

The air weighed around me as if a ton of bricks smashed through the inside of my stomach and the very acid now leaked and spread its choking fumes.

Clip after clip rolled, utter normality with hints of human slaughter. Together the family grew, laughed, dined. Ashta became 15, 16, 17, discovering the divine hobby of human torture, or to them "playing with the livestock" 18, 19, 20. The present. A clip of her splashing in fresh blood as if it were a puddle, pushing her brother. Holding her stomach from the laughter of seeing him pretending to swim in it. The same way we laughed at narwhals.

Sibling fun. The movie ended.

"That was last week," the purple eyed man smiled, reminiscing.

Numbness crashed down on me as if gravity itself had decided to leave the world be and focus its strength on crushing me. The irrational thoughts I had pushed down burst out through every pore on my body. "How was the meal?" The man smiled.

"What is it?" I finally whispered, my eyes stuck on the small piece left on my plate.

"It's my sisters favourite food.."

"What is it?" I whispered again, tears gushing uncontrollably down my face.

"Ins my darling," he grinned.

"What is it!!" I screamed, my eyes bloodshot.

"Darling," he smiled amused, "it's human."

I slumped down in my chair. My body demanding to puke but with neither energy nor anything in my stomach to free. Tears burned the hole inside me into a true void. A void of never ending hatred, a void of fear, a void of anger, a void of... acceptance.

"Bring her," I whispered half heartedly, my body like a rag doll.

"Who?"

"Ashta."

"Why?"

"I don't believe you."

To this, he burst into a throat chortling cackle. "You know what? You truly might just be an A+ ins."

"What?" I ask in disgust, barely raising my head.

"Well you probably already know that A and A+ ins is only a myth, but you, you my darling, far surpass such a rare idea! You know what? I'm feeling kind. Let me ask you a few questions and I'll bring you Ashta, ok?"

I did not reply.

"Ok then, what powers do you have?"

"I don't have any," I said clenching my teeth I tried to keep my head above the crashing waves on nausea.

"Don't lie to me," he snapped.

"I am not,"

"How did you run off so fast from me?"

"What?"

"In that street, the first time I saw you, how were you so fast?"

"I have no idea what you're talking about," I slurred as sharp dagger like pains stabbed at my head.

"Fine, I won't bring Ashta," he crossed his arms.

"I'm not lying. I don't know what your talking about..."

"You ran with incredible speed! I had been watching you before, you could barely walk! How did you run so fast?!" He shouted, anger spitting from his mouth.

"I was afraid," I whispered.

"What?"

"Afraid!"

"Your power is fear," he rolled his eyes.

"I don't have powers! I was just afraid," I sobbed dejectedly without tears, "adrenaline took over."

"Aha! Who's adrenaline?"

"What?"

"Who is she?" His eyes widened in greed.

"It's not a person," I answered.

"So it's?"

"You don't have adrenaline?' I tried, and failed, to lift my head as I asked bewilderedly.

"What. Is. It." He prowled closer, almost foaming at the mouth.

"It's a hormone."

"Ok?"

"Fight or flight... Gets the body ready for danger, muscles ready for exertion, faster blood circulation, faster breath?"

"So, it is true."

I stay silent, the explanation having sucked the life out of me.

"Humans *are* the fifth dimas," he murmured to himself, then looked straight at me "but you're not like the humans here..."

Getting up he stares at me with his eyes of pure purple smoke, intensifying the colour of his hair, those shards of ice. "I will get Ashta as promised, wait until you hear about her plans to farm your world" he chuckled and left, locking the door behind him.

Farm my world...

Chapter 27

Half an hour later, as I drowned in the waves of silence, the unlocking of the door pulled me out of my hypnotic state like a suffocating fish out of water. The door, however, did not open.

A strange urge to get up washed over me, picking me off the chair and pushing me towards the door. My hand laid on the strangely cold door handle. Creek, the handle began to push itself, my hand merely a decoration on its icy facade.

The hallway stood in front of me, a silent oasis, no one standing, no one waiting. For a slight second, I thought to return back to my seat to wait for Ashta but logic quickly took over. That same logic then turned against me, convincing me it was a trap and yet, a strange gut feeling whispered to me otherwise.

The door. A door of which could lead to the heavens above or the depths of hell, with a carpet of polar opposites connecting between the two worlds, sanity and insanity, yet the edges lay bare, masking which is which.

I took a step. Then, another. Blinded by something. Another step. Something profound yet not something I could grasp. Another step. The answers that simply cannot exist. Another step. Sweat ran down my neck as I fully embraced the calls.

Steps turned into a walk then broke into a run. The walls began to cave in on me or perhaps it was the muscles of my body contracting, pushing, caving in, crushing the very bones of which begged for release.

No directions and yet the walls seemed to guide me. The same walls started to grow lava red eyes, begging for something but only having the ability to communicate through those said eyes.

The eyes cried, sobbed. Tears of blood stained the pristine walls. Silent and yet deafeningly screaming. Following my movement, moving left to right as I pass by. Everyone was gone. No life existed, not even myself. I was merely a figment of those bloodied eyes. Those blood crying eyes. Eyes. Eyes!

The deer. Red. Red. Red. In a fog, no, *it was* the fog, it's eyes glowed in every direction, gleaming everywhere and yet nowhere. Blood! The slow pour of scorching lava after an explosion.

Red became my vision, a thick honey like vision, a vision of beginning, of the end. Thick droplets rained from the ceiling, red, red blood. Sweetly seeping into my mouth and intertwining with my tongue. *Am I red?*

Out the abandoned doors, through the grounds housing those lush flowers, dead as the world around me. Red. Red. Red. *Am I blood?*

It stood there.

It stood, waiting.

The creature.

The monster.

Its rumbled breaths vibrating with my own, "what are you?" I asked a single tear rolling down my eye, not out of fear, not of anger, but of understanding.

It did not answer but turned and ran. My legs feebly tried to catch up as they watched its bizarre spider-like body heave over the ground. The deer ran besides me. The world, a blur of paint on a canvas, getting redder and redder. A type of red unseen, unheard of.

I raised my hand to my face to wipe the tears that seemed to seep. I was met with a hand of blood. Pure thick blood. Tears of blood.

The deer disappeared, no, for I was the deer! my eyes bleeding out what can never be said!

I ran. Ran as I raised my bloody hands to touch the trees that seemed to have sprouted from nowhere, leaving my mark, traces of my existence. The lushes green leaves that once glimmered and glowed as if they absorb the eternal peace and happiness of the sun, now overdosing on my delusions. Glistening with red.

Each foot that hit the ground surged with profound energy perhaps I was even flying. "Haha! My little spider friend!" I screamed to the wind, to the clouds, to the skies as they melted into the thickness of red. The miraculous red! Blood! Blood! Blood!

Her highness stood in front of me! I curtseyed while I ran. An elegant run of bouncing the knees simultaneously and lowering the back to show respect! The queen still stood in between her royal guards, her intricate wood body decorated by her leafy hair, surrounded by the giant tree guards. The tree!

She stood mystically, her beauty still containing the door that stood in the middle of her. Though this time, instead of it radiating a pastel yellow with passionate red swirls in the corners, the colours were inverted, swapped for the door to be mostly covered by the vivid human colours of blood and hints of yellow! Yellow? No! red!

"Red! Red! Red!" I roared with understanding.

In, out, it was all the same, an imprisonment bound upon us by this earth. Coming out of the tree, sparks began to burn the inside of my body, the world getting smaller, the once giant trees nothing more than funny pieces of broccoli, the monster a game, a bizarre-looking toy, a weak little rag doll.

I ran. We ran. We all ran. Blanketed but the warmth of blood. My head nearly reached the trees. The monster's legs began to fall, flying behind it like long twigs, like amusing confetti celebrating such a beautiful bloodied day. Red! Only two of its legs remained as we ran through a minuscule meadow with what seemed to be incredibly small flowers, nearly invisible to the naked-eyed. Then there it stood, the illusion of belonging, home!

My own body seemed to pick up rapid speed, the wind lashed at my face as my eyes framed my house. Hurdling, almost gliding, at a speed I never noticed I had, I ran and ran as if my life depended on it.

Relief, the feeling absorbed me. My soul intertwined with tears of joy. Home! Oh, how much had I yearned, how much had I begged?! The very meadow wrapped its grass blanket around me, seeping the warmth of consolation. Home! Home! Home!

Tears stormed down my face forming puddles as I ran, the valves of my heart unscrewing as it overflowed with ecstasy. As if I had grown more legs, the earth rumbled beneath me, nothing having the ability to stand in my way. *Home. Finally home!*

The monster now had become the size of a person and seemed to have begun to slow down, its eyes stuck on the house door. It grabbed the doorknob and entered as I roared for it to stop.

"HOME!" I screamed manically, my eyes on the verge of falling out of its sockets.

I stood outside, the house seemed to have shrunk, the top of the door standing at my stomach.

"Home?" I whispered, my breath becoming heavy.

I looked through my bedroom window but was met with darkness. "Mum!" I cried, like the cries of a hungry hatchling, except starving for the heartbeats of my mother in the arms of home.

I picked up a pebble, my fingers felt weak, and threw it against my window, "please," I implored, tears begging to escape but not finding a way out.

I threw some again.

Tap. Tap. Tap.

And again.

Tap. Tap. Tap.

And again, till a girl peeked out the window, fear suddenly electrocuting her. "LEAVE!" I boomed, "LEAVE!" continuing to throw pebbles.

Tap. Tap. Tap.

Something bizarre glimmered next to her, something spine-chilling, petrifying. A mirror. A reflection.

Tap. Tap. Tap.

A reflection of my surroundings but with a gruesome thing standing in the middle.

Tap. Tap. Tap.
Heaving up and down.
Tap. Tap. Tap
A monster.
Tap. Tap. Tap.
The spider monster.
Tap. Tap. Tap.
My reflection?
Tap. Tap. Tap.
I do not know why I have been writing this.
Tap. Tap. Tap
Was I not the deer?
Tap. Tap. Tap.
The slab of meat?
Tap. Tap. Tap.
The monster?
Tap. Tap. Tap.
It is not the human race who is weak, it is whatever I am that is weak, at least that thought is what keeps me sane. The circle of life seems so meaningless when you are a mere spectator, one who does not get brutally dragged down and forced to live through the same torture again and again will not fully understand. Life is a paradox and one cannot comprehend this until they're stuck in the middle.
Tap. Tap. Tap.
Resistance is futile.
Tap. Tap. Tap.
There's no running away from it.
Tap. Tap. Tap.
That is the sound you hear once the devil decides to use you as his little toy.
Tap. Tap. Tap

...

About The Author

Lujayne Alqefari is a profound writer from Saudi Arabia. As well as being a passionate writer with a BA in Languages and Translation, she dabbles in poetry, art, philosophy, and all things knowledge. She began writing her first novel, *A Passing Red*, at the age of 18 and plans to write many more.

www.ingramcontent.com/pod-product-compliance
Lightning Source LLC
LaVergne TN
LVHW091441190726
843491LV00007B/1833